MOURNING WAFFLES

AN UMA BLANCHARD COZY MYSTERY

Mourning Waffles: An Uma Blanchard Cozy Mystery
Copyright © 2025 by Trixie Fairdale
Rusty Ogre Publishing
www.rustyogrepublishing.com
Casper, WY, USA

All Rights Reserved.

No part of this book may be reproduced in any manner, or transmitted in any form or by any means, electronic, mechanical, photocopying, recording or otherwise, without express written permission by the author(s) and or publisher, except for the use of a brief quotation in a book review.

This book is a work of fiction.
Names, characters, places, events, organizations and incidents are either part of the author's imagination or are used fictitiously. Any resemblance to actual persons, living or dead, or actual events is purely coincidental.

Cover Art by Erica Summers

ISBN: 9781962854504

1

Festive zydeco seeps from a portable speaker hanging from a branch in one of my lemon trees. The cheery accordion oozes through spring air perfumed by citrus blossoms and Old Bay.

"How are you even *doing* that?" Jacoby mutters, mouth slung open in shock like he's watching me answer a Mensa-level equation.

"Doin' what?" I wipe juice from my chin with the back of my hand. *Oh, mercy, these hands.* Wrinkled. Battle-worn. Age-spotted to the point that I look like a Holstein. I remember when they used to hold Harry's glock as still as a statue when we'd take the *pirogue* down into the Blind River Bayou for some afternoon target practice.

Now, I can't even hold a darned *mudbug* without shakin' like a bank teller mid-robbery.

"I'm not getting diddley-squat out of mine, Gran." Jacoby tosses his crawfish down petulantly in the square hole carved out of the middle of my custom cypress table.

Harold made it himself; *God rest his sweet soul.* He cut the whole table out of a single tree trunk his father felled near his family's pond out in Saint Amant. He was always so talented. You could give that man a hammer and some nails, and he'll build you an Antebellum palace in a month.

"Here." I snatch a fist-sized crawfish out from a mountain of spiced corn and potatoes and lob it at Jacoby. Then, I fish out another for myself. "And don't call me *Gran.*"

"Oh. Well… What should I call you?" One of his bushy black eyebrows creeps up his forehead. Kid's six-foot-whatever and a dead-ringer for his dad -- *much to his misfortune* -- only with a thick head'a hair. Same Rudolph bulb at the end of his nose. Same turned-in front teeth like the *Buc-ee's Beaver.* Same chubby cheeks. Same weak, nonexistent chin. Boy's the spittin' image of Carl, I tell ya. All Jacoby's missing is his daddy's mess of random tattoos, the scraggly tuft of beard, and the chrome-dome that makes his father look like a peach turtle.

Cripes, the *glare* off that thing…

"How's-about some *lagniappe*, huh? Gimme a nickname that's a little somethin' special."

"What about Gran-Gran?" Jacoby shrugs, suspiciously eyeing his crawfish like it's about to magically come back to life in his hand.

I sigh. This boy's about as dense as cypress wood. Definitely gets *that* from his father. The apple don't fall far from the tree. I watched Carl try to build a crib a few months back. Shoulda filmed it. The shabby little thing fell apart in two days without anything even *in* it. Thank God the baby hadn't come yet.

"Kid, if I didn't like 'Gran,' why would I like being called the same thing *twice*?"

He shrugs.

"Now what? You're almost twenty. How's-about you just call me by my name, hmmm?"

"Uma?" His brown eyes squint quizzically.

I holler over the shoulder pads of my short-sleeved sweater at one of my daughters. "Ding-ding-ding! Someone get this kid a prize!"

His shoulders slump at the ribbing. Maybe I should go easy on him. I know my blood turns to ice every time I think about Carl being legally related to *me* in less than a week. I can't imagine how much worse it's gotta be to be blood kin to the man.

"Yes, you can call me Uma. Okay," I widen my stance and roll my shoulders back like I'm about to embark on some sort of athletic feat. That would be quite a sight, seein' as though I can't even squat down to pick something off the floor without my hips crackin' ten times. Sounds like rotted wood popping on a campfire every time I put on my socks. "What you wanna *do* is pinch here on the little chest plate and rip this sucker in half." I illustrate this with my own crawfish, like a flight stewardess with over-the-top hand gestures.

"Then, ya gon' pinch the tail at the flipper right here and pull the meat out with those two front beaver teeth, like so," I say, pointing to the spot where the segments of the tail meet the tiny red flipper.

"*Ma*," Jolene warns, flashing me a harsh glance at how I just talked to her future stepson.

I nod at Jacoby, a weak attempt at a non-verbal apology. Then, I illustrate how to pluck the meat out, feeling the pull of my dentures against the roof of my mouth. I miss my old teeth, but after all the sugary drive-through daiquiris I've sucked back and pieces of praline pie I've bulldozed through, in retrospect, I don't really regret a thing. *Worth it.*

Jacoby struggles with the juicy, dripping decapod, mangling the crustacean's lower half with his teeth to get at the heavenly bit of meat inside.

"Takes a bit of practice getting used to it. You're halfway there," I say, attempting to be encouraging.

"This is a lot of work for so little meat," he mutters in frustration, looking at the remnants of the tail in his glistening palm.

I don't respond.

He's a Yankee. What can ya do?

C'est la vie.

"Put the other side to your mouth. Inhale real hard and suck the head."

"Ew!" Jacoby grimaces, peering into the dead, black eyes of the halved creature in his mitt.

"Oh, *please*." Roxanne, my eldest, says to him with an eye roll. Her husband, Lenny, snickers and sweeps some empty tails through the table's hole with an outstretched pinky.

"No, not '*Ew*,'" I say. "The head's where all the fats'n juices are! Don't even *think* about calling ya'self part of this family if you ain't suckin' the heads, *cher*."

I want to pinch the bridge of my nose in anger at the kid, but I don't. It'll just lead to me gettin' Old Bay in my eyes for the umpteenth time. My vision's poor enough without addin' spices to the mix.

"Once you've sucked the head, jus' chuck it in the hole." I loudly slurp the contents of the one in my hand and chuck the spent top half of the ten-legged crustacean in the hole. It quietly clicks against the mound of prior casualties in the trash can positioned beneath.

Jacoby follows my order and bobbles his head. "Okay, that wasn't as bad as I thought."

"Not that *bad*? Hun, this 'dis-here's like *gold*," Roxanne says firmly.

Lenny flashes a smile and then speaks. A rarity. "I love watchin' you Yanks attempt Cajun traditions. We gotta get 'dis boy a king cake while he's down here."

Lenny's like a big ol' Golden Retriever. He doesn't bring a lot of smarts to the table, but he's loyal to Roxanne somethin' fierce. And just like a Retriever, he's always fetchin' my rubbish bin from the street when he comes over. And he brings my paper in from the stoop like a good boy. As long as the man don't tinkle on my floors or drool on my furniture, he's a welcome addition to the family.

...Unlike Jacoby's daddy, Carl.

"Yeah, I jus' love watchin' them struggle to keep the powdered sugar from their *beignets* off of their shirts," one of my other daughters, Maggie May, says. She ended up spendin' a lotta time down in Thibodaux after high school and ended up with a southern drawl thicker'n the rest of my kids.

Maggie's girlfriend, Whitney, chimes in. "Not nearly as fun as hearin' 'em try to spell the word *Natchitoches*, though. Or heck, even to say the *word* Louisiana."

"When someone says that word any way other than *Lose-yanna,* you jus' *know* they ain't from 'round here," Roxanne says with a laugh.

"Or when they say New Or-leans." Lenny chuckles. Everyone knows it's pronounced with two lazy syllables. *Naw-lins.* Say it any way other'n that and you'll get corrected by a local.

Jacoby starts tearing into another crawfish. He yanks the tiny wad of spiced meat out, whips his head back, and gobbles it like a seal eating a sardine.

Jacoby seems like a nice enough kid. Little needy, but his father, Carl, up-and-bolted after he impregnated Jacoby's mother, so the story goes. His daddy gets around. He's a walkin' red flag. I wish I coulda steered Jolene away, but she's always been a stubborn girl. Pushin' her to leave Carl this close to the wedding would only make her double down, I'm sure.

I just gotta let this thing run its course like I did with her last baby's daddy.

Excited that he successfully extracted a tail, Jacoby yells over his shoulder. "Dad! Come here!"

Carl ignores the request from my back patio. He's leaning against the wooden fence on the far side of the yard, shotgunning a warm can of Busch and talking to a couple over the Morning Glory-covered chain link. These people must be my new neighbors. I saw a U-haul truck in the driveway yesterday. Hours later, a flock of pink plastic flamingos and various owl and pineapple figurines were already littering their lawn.

Carl laughs at something the neighbor says. As much as I hate the man, he's admittedly got a disarming charm that makes people feel like he's a friend. I don't buy the sincerity of it for one second, but I can see how my most naive and wayward daughter became so enamored with him after such a short time.

Now that she's gone and *bred* with him, I s'pose I best give the guy a chance. Maybe by the time the baby comes,

I'll be able to speak to the idiot without wantin' to wring the neck buried beneath that weak chin 'a his.

"Dad!" Jacoby yells again.

Once more, Carl ignores his adult son like a ghost in a nineties Shyamalan flick. He chugs the last of his foamy beer and stomps the empty flat, leaving a ring of wetness on the porch I just had my neighbor across the street power-wash for me.

Carl's head whirls toward us. A brief glimmer of hope flits in Jacoby's eyes. "Jolene, babe, come over here. Meet the neighbors." He waves my youngest over, flinging wet droplets of Busch with every theatrical hand movement. "C'mon. Chop-chop."

Jolene flashes Jacoby an apologetic expression and rubs her protruding belly as she waddles across the grass, dodging my landscaped clusters of colorful lantanas. The poor girl's gotta somehow fit in a wedding dress in a few days, and she looks like she swallowed a basketball without chewing. She's only seven months along. By the time she's ready to give birth, she's gonna be the size of an Endymion Mardi Gras float.

"Today, please." Carl whips his hand in a big circle. Her stride is too slow for his liking.

My faux molars grind. With a family as big as mine, there are bound to be a few rotten apples in the bunch. This one is just a three-hundred-and-thirty-*pound* apple covered in ugly tattoos of Egyptian symbols, half-naked pin-ups, and a compass with no directions. How fitting. I knew he was directionless after talkin' with him ten minutes. I didn't need to see it indelibly advertised on the side'a his neck to get the picture!

"When's Daniel and Jane coming?" Roxanne asks, snapping me out of my little trance.

"They ain't," I say before popping a piece of boiled celery in my mouth and sucking juice from my wrinkly thumb. "Twins had karate today. Their parents drove 'em all the way out to Chalmette for it."

"What? That's crazy," Roxanne says with a furrowed brow. "There's a dojo right around the corner from their house!"

"That's not what's crazy. What's *crazy* is they're teaching those little demons to fight even better'n they already do!"

"Mom, you shouldn't call your grandbabies *demons*," Roxanne warns gently.

"They are! You ever babysat those boys? 'Cause I have! Last time, they nearly singed my eyebrows off with the fire they built in the garage. Melted a whole stack 'a five-gallon buckets I used to use to plant my veggies. *Those kids are evil, I tell ya!* I wasn't but ten minutes into my program when I smelled the smoke."

"Well, maybe you shouldn't be watchin' murder shows while you're babysittin'."

"Who said it was a murder show?" I howl.

"Mother, that's *all* you watch," Maggie May chirps. "The twins don't need to see people gettin' found in dumpsters all bloody and whatnot."

"You're probably right 'bout that. It might start givin' 'em too many ideas!"

"No, I meant, you should be out flyin' kites with 'em or readin' them something."

"First off, when was the last time we had enough wind in Killjoy for kite-flyin', hmm? Secondly, the last time I *did* fly a kite with them, they tried to use the cord to string up the neighbor's Persian. By the time I caught up to 'em, they had that poor cat hog-tied already! God knows what those little demons would have *done to it* had I not intervened. I'm tellin' you, they're a future serial killer duo. Henry Lee Lucas and Ottis Toole, I tell ya."

Jacoby gnaws another little lump of meat out of a crawfish. "Got another one!"

"Dey you go, kid." I pat Jacoby on the back to subtly wipe my hand on his shirt.

"Good job," Roxanne says, pointing to the back door. "If you get tired of crawfish, there's jambalaya over there in the crock. Mom makes the best."

She's not wrong. *I really do.*

"Roxy's right. Can't go wrong with our mother's jambalaya," Maggie May adds.

Yes, if you're keeping track, my kids are Roxanne, Jolene, Maggie May, Mandy, and Daniel. Am I a fan of seventies and eighties rock music? *You bet your booty, I am*. Named 'em all after songs I liked. Some people think it's silly, but I think what Jolene named *her* firstborn is what's downright ridiculous.

Payzlee.

Ugh. Can you imagine not only growing up named after a *hideous* design but to then have the bastardized spelling of it look on paper like a spilled bowl of alphabet soup? I'll take my Elton John and Dolly Parton references *any* day.

"Uma, stop being antisocial and come over here and meet your new neighbors," Carl barks at me from across the yard.

This forty-two-year-old man-child has some nerve…

I toss down the crawfish in my hand and point at Jacoby. "Don't fill up on dem crawfish, *cher*. I actually *do* have a king cake inside for dessert."

"Is it even *possible* to fill up on crawfish?" Jacoby jokes.

I throw him a sour glance and shuffle over to Carl and Jolene, taking my sweet time.

I haven't even gotten all the way over when Carl starts yapping. "Uma. These are your new neighbors, Matt and Belinda Guidry."

Matt's hand juts out over the fence, clearly eager to shake mine. I take it reluctantly, trying my best to plaster on a charming smile.

"Uma Blanchard." I grab his hand hard before he has the chance to vice-grip me first. He looks strong, biceps bulging out from beneath the sleeves of a polo. On one of his arms is a tattoo of an upside-down pineapple. "I see you both have a lot in common already."

I point to the pineapple and then to the off-kilter ankh on Carl's meaty calf, the lop-sided ink design peeking out below his stained khaki shorts. "Y'all both had the same drunk tattoo artist."

Matt laughs with his whole diaphragm. "No, ma'am, it's intended to be upside-down."

Jolene leans toward my ear and whispers, *"I'll tell you what it means later."*

I nod almost imperceptibly and force a smile, a polite southern nicety that has been ingrained in me since childhood. "So, Matt, where'd you move here from?"

"Florida," Belinda finally speaks, "right smack in the middle. Little town called Ocala."

"Down by dat retirement community where all them STDs are spreadin'?"

Matt laughs again, nervously this time. "Yeah, 'bout thirty minutes drive from the Oaks, but… worry not. I assure you, we're disease-free. Regularly tested."

"*Ohhhh-kay*," I grumble.

Odd response, but whatever.

"Well, welcome to Killjoy. Y'all want a bowl of jambalaya? Or some boudin? I always cook up too much."

"No, we're all set. Thank you, Ms. Blanchard," Matt speaks for the both of them.

The woman speaks now. Belinda, or whatever. "So... do you have parties like this all the time... or...?"

I laugh. This is *hardly* what I'd call a party. We Cajuns pretty much *invented* the word, after all. "Yeah. We feed the strays constantly."

That makes Matt chuckle. He's quite handsome. Why couldn't my daughter have found someone like this young buck to settle down with?

"Well, now, Ma, this *is* a bit of a special occasion," Jolene says, clutching Carl's tattooed arm to her. "Carl and I are getting' hitched in three days."

"Oh! Congratulations!" Belinda chirps.

"*Third time's a charm*, I guess." My words are laced with more salt than *andouille* sausage as I glare up at my future son-in-law.

I hate that Jolene'll be his *third wife*. The man is bad news. Sure, Jolene is no saint, and she has a two-year-old child outta wedlock with another man, but she's still too good for *this* chuckle-head.

Rumor has it he's done slept his way through half of *Orleans Parish* already.

"Oh, you." Carl puts his meaty arm around me and gives my shoulders a playful squeeze. I'm sure he'd love to keep squeezing until he hears something *snap*.

In three days, they'll be married, and this waste of flesh'll officially be kin to me.

Thankfully, in *four* days, I can drink all my troubles away as I sip my fifth mojito of the afternoon on the lido of the new Oshannic Aspire, as it carries me and thousands of other vacationers out of the Port of New Orleans.

Ahhhh, five days of uninterrupted bliss where I can let myself forget about Jolene's Chantilly cake, iris bouquets, seatin' arrangements, and that butt-ugly groomsman cake Carl wanted in the shape of a feral hog.

The man's got zero taste, I tell ya.

2

I stuff two short-sleeved sweaters in my suitcase and stare, wonderin' if it will even be cold enough on the cruise at any point to wear 'em. I imagine it'll be freezin' in the dance club, the casino, the formal dinin' room, and most importantly, the karaoke hall. Surely, at least one floor'll be blastin' the A.C. enough to warrant some elegant cashmere.

Cocodrie, my ancient chihuahua, watches from my pillow through fogged eyes full of cataracts. He lets out a little grunt of disapproval, sharp teeth of his under-bite pulled into a silly sneer.

"Hey, Bud, I'm not askin' you to be happy for me. Lord knows you aren't happy about anything. But you should be thankin' me! You get to go see your girlfriend at Cosmo's house."

As I shuffle through the formal wear buried in the back of my closet, I think about Cosmo Goodman and get a little warm all over. I stuff two long gowns and a cocktail dress in my suitcase and walk over to the window. I peer across the street at Cosmo's house. The light to his bedroom is on, and I feel a little flutter of excitement in my belly at the thought of him looking out and catchin' me starin'. There is an image of him in my mind, shirtless, chest and arms as muscular as he was in the last film I saw him in.

See, Cosmo spent forty years in the film industry as a stunt double who stayed in incredibly high demand. Even now, I'm sure he could throw himself at the hood of a movin' car, glance off the top, tumble onto the pavement, and get back up without so much as bloodyin' a lip.

From my satin pillowcase, still curled up like a li'l tan bean, Cocodrie lets out another gurgle of irritation at my unabashed ogling.

I'm just about to evict the furry alligator from my pillow so I can get some shut-eye when I see a beat-up pickup truck aggressively pull up in front 'a my house. It's an old red Dodge with a canary-yellow scrape across the passenger door like someone grazed a concrete pillar in a grocery store parkin' lot with it.

The person behind the wheel throws it into park and gets out. It's dark, but the figure looks like a man, tall and imposin', lumberin' toward my front door!

Moments later, I hear the poundin' *rat-tat-tat* of a meaty fist on wood. I look down at the smartwatch on my wrist, one my son Daniel got me for Christmas... so's I could watch my heart rate spike in times like these, I suppose.

It's 10:38 p.m.

Who in God's-good-name is comin' to my front door and makin' such a ruckus at nearly eleven o'clock at night on a Tuesday?

Rat-tat-tat again against the wood. The unwanted visitor sounds absolutely furious.

"Open the door, Carl! I know you're in there!" His booming voice pours in plain-as-day through the screen of my open window. I have no idea what to do. I stand frozen, thinking about Jolene and the baby. I hear Payzlee cry somewhere on the other side of the house.

"Come out, you coward! Act like a man for once in your life!" The sound booms across my quiet neighborhood. Cosmo's formidable silhouette fills the window now as he peels open his blinds to watch the commotion. I can't help but notice he's as shirtless as I imagined.

I hear the door finally open. Carl's voice growls, "What?!"

"Really? Jolene's not enough? You gotta take what's *mine* now, too?" The man hollers it with pain in his voice.

"You can't be here, man. This is my mother-in-law's house! People are getting ready for bed."

"I don't care who I wake up!" the man screams, louder now. "You ruined my life! Do you even care? We were like brothers!"

"Listen," Carl says, trying to calm the man, "I can explain. What *exactly* did she tell you?"

"Babe, who is it?" The voice is Jolene's now. I'd know it anywhere.

Payzlee cries harder.

"Go! Just *go*, Jolene."

"I'm not going anywhere," she says defiantly. *Atta girl!*

"Jolene, please! This doesn't concern you."

"Oh," the stranger says with a pained laugh, "it certainly does concern you, Jolene. Do you know where Carl's been every Tuesday afternoon while I've been in relationship counseling, trying to save my marriage?"

"No," she says timidly.

"Bro, please. Go home and cool down. You're angry. I get that—"

"Don't you *dare* tell *me* to calm down. And don't ever call me *bro* again, you snake!"

"Answer the question. Where *has* he been? I thought he was takin' a martial arts class," Jolene says.

"Oh, he's been wrestling and pinning someone, alright! My *wife*!"

"Carl! What the…? Is he tellin' the truth?"

There's a long pause where that bald rat is tryin' to think his way outta the pit he done dug himself.

"We just had a child! Is…" The man starts to cry. "Is it even mine?"

I hear Carl sigh, and my eyes drift back to Cosmo. He sees me and waves.

"Is my son even mine, Carl?" The man growls, and suddenly, I hear Jolene scream. Then, I hear the sound of a fist collidin' with something hard. Payzlee screeches, and a body tumbles to the cypress floorboards in the entryway.

Jolene yips. "Oh my God, are you okay?!"

I see the darkened stranger stalk through my grass with purpose, tramplin' through the ornamental grass just beyond the giant magnolia tree in the front yard.

He whips around and points back at the doorway. "You're gonna pay for this, Carl! You're gon' wish you never stepped foot into my life!"

With that, the man hoists himself into his pickup, cranks the engine, and roars down the street.

3

Twenty minutes later, I lug my burstin' suitcase outta my room, struggling with the cumbersome bag every doggone inch of the way, clumsily bashin' it against every narrow doorjamb in the house.

"Little help here?" I say as I enter the kitchen and look at the two irritated people sitting in it. Jolene is starin' out the window at the breakfast nook, bitin' her lip like she is tryin' to tunnel her way through it with her teeth. Carl's in a chair, head back, hunk'a red meat draped over his left eye.

Jolene rises awkwardly from her chair, pregnant belly first. "Here, Ma, let me get that for you."

I pull it away. "No. Not you."

"I'm busy," Carl mutters. I can hear how swollen his nose is as he speaks.

"So you wanna stay rent-free at *my* house, never do dishes, never help my daughter a lick with her firstborn, and *then*," I yank the steak off his face and hold it up in the air, "you're gonna take my thick-cut rib-eye out the fridge and use it as an ice pack? Then, you're gonna have the *gall* to not even bother to help?"

He snatches the meat out of my hand angrily and slaps it back on his eye without a word.

"What are you even doin', Ma? Is that for the cruise?" Jolene glances down at my stuffed suitcase.

"Yeah," I say, glowering down at Carl, even though he can't see me through the beautifully marbled meat.

"It's not for a few more days," Jolene says, like I've suddenly gone senile. Like I don't even know what day it is.

"That's correct." I roll my eyes. "But I heard dat little tiff on the porch y'all just had… You know, the one that just woke up half the neighborhood? I figured, now that the weddin's off, I'd get a li'l jump on things."

"What do you mean?" Jolene asks defensively. "No one's called the weddin' off."

"Oh, dear God, Jolene. I heard it. We *all* heard it. Seems half the *town* just heard Carl can't control that little Carl's Junior burger in his pants. You're not still goin' through with this li'l *sham*, are you?"

"*Sham?*" They both say in unison, offended in tandem.

"Jolene, you've got strange men comin' to the door… *my* door… tellin' you that Carl has been unfaithful. You're not seriously gonna walk down that aisle!"

"Ma! Carl's relatives have flown in from all over. He's got family already checked into their hotels. What are we supposed to tell 'em?"

"The *truth*, Jolene." I stubbornly drag my suitcase out the front door to a porch that's seen as much violence tonight as the stage on the *Springer* Show. One of the wheels catches on a fractured paver, and I nearly topple over. The heft of the bag probably weighs more'n I do.

"Hold on, Sweetness," a voice hollers from across the street, and I smile. "Lemme help."

Cosmo Goodman's strong hands clasp around the handle of my bag, and he tugs it right outta the hole it's stuck in. He lifts it with ease, and I follow, studying the curves of his shirtless chest. He's barefoot, wearing only a pair of silly pajama pants with illustrations of little Cavalier King Charles Spaniels all over them. They sit just at the base of his still-defined abs. I am in awe of how devilishly good he looks for sixty-eight.

"What was all that madness about earlier?" he asks.

"I heard about as much as you did. I wish I could say I'm shocked, but in the past year, I've heard rumblings about Carl's reputation."

"He a real floozy?" Cosmo asks, a charming smile creepin' up onto his handsome face. His cheeks have stubble, a sort of five o'clock shadow I'm not used to seein' on his normally clean-cut self. *Lord have mercy,* his dimples make my knees weaker'n they already *are* at my age.

"Yeah, you could say that." I chuckle.

Cosmo reaches the driveway and holds my bag up effortlessly as we near the car. "You skippin' town early? Drivin' Jolene in this-here getaway vehicle?"

"I *wish*." I scoff as I pull out my keys, a metal ring with a heavy Bachman Turner Overdrive keychain adorning it. I unlock the trunk of my Buick. Cosmo sets the suitcase inside, and I close it, leaning against my trunk to steady myself in his presence.

"Jolene just made it clear that she intends to go through with this travesty," I say, fighting the urge to roll my eyes so hard that I pull a muscle behind one.

"Oh no, really?"

"I wish I knew voodoo at times like these. I'd stab a pin right into that doll's bald head and spare my daughter the future decades with him."

"Oof. Havin' to watch that kinda stuff as a parent is rougher'n a cat's tongue." He crosses his arms in front of his chest, and it only makes his pecs look even more muscular. I have to stop myself from starin'.

"I just wish this idiot was gone forever. Know what I'm sayin'?" I elbow him and feel a zing of excitement as my arm brushes his bare skin.

"Hey, don't look at *me*. My days of playin' a hitman are over." He snickers. "Unless, of course, I get a call from Clint Eastwood about bein' a stunt double for him in another one of his self-directed action dramas."

"Heck, I wouldn't have the money to pay you anyway." I laugh.

"Well, Ms. Blanchard, you sleep well tonight. Tomorrow's a brand new day. It'll all work out. You'll see." Cosmo winks, and I feel my heart palpitate. "Night, darlin'."

"See you in a few days when I drop off Cocodrie."

He nods, tipping his head like some respectful cowboy, and my mind instantly flashes back to a western drama he was in in the eighties, ridin' a brown mare, shirt half-buttoned, youthful face as serious as a heart attack.

...*Maybe I watched it a few times.*

...Maybe it's in my DVD player *right now.*

...Maybe I already know *exactly* how many minutes into the movie his short scene is.

4

At seven a.m., my eyes shoot open in bed. I don't even need to set the alarm anymore. My body's internal clock keeps time like a Rolex, smooth and reliable. My dreams were restless. Around four o'clock in the morning, I even had one that ended in the stranger pounding on my door again as hard as he possibly could. It woke me up in a panic. Cocodrie started yappin' simultaneously. It took a few minutes to get back to sleep.

The sun is already slicin' through the blinds, and the birds are having a field day in the magnolia tree outside my bathroom window. I glue in my dentures and toss on a new robe, one adorned with citrus fruits all over it. I think about my upcomin' cruise and grin at the thought of it.

"Couple more days," I mumble to myself.

I can almost taste the ice-cold Mexican margaritas and feel the dry heat sizzlin' on my thin skin already. The only question now is, what excursions do I want to do on the days I'm docked in Cozumel and the Yucatan? So many options. Parasailing, spelunking, cave exploration, tourin' Mayan ruins, swimmin' with the dolphins…

Maybe I'll do a few. *YOLO*, as my grandson Stokely always says, usually before thrusting his twin brother head-first into the street. Kid's evil, I tell ya.

I hear a loud *ding* of something that sounds like it's comin' from across the house. I'm probably not the first up. Especially if Carl was still gonna go catfishing on Bayou Segnette this morning. He'd been talkin' about it long before he used my seventeen-dollar steak as an eyepatch.

I make my way through the house, knees clickin' like plastic cogs that don't line up right. All I can think about is the hazelnut coffee with milk my body so desperately craves, special-ordered java grounds so caffeinated they could reanimate a long-dead corpse like Lazarus.

I catch a whiff of somethin' sweet as I waltz through the living room, walls painted coral with sea foam green furniture and dust-free white statuettes on doilies adornin' every flat surface. Fresh white day lilies sit in vases all around my livin' room. I grow 'em myself in my garden in the back.

But this smell ain't the lilies *or* my cafe *au lait*. It's a curious combination. It smells like pancake batter, syrup, and… something *metallic.*

Copper, maybe?

Jolene comes out of the guest room with Payzlee wrapped around her swollen torso like a spider monkey with only *marginally* less hair. Kid was born with a head of it so thick the Audubon Zoo wanted her for their primate exhibit.

Jolene yawns and gives half a wave, bright blue eyes barely open. "Hey, Ma."

"Hey, *ma belle*." I kiss her on the cheek. "Want some coffee?"

"Wish I could." She manages a smile, soul heavy from the heft of her bloated belly and the weight of the second child atop it. She follows me into the kitchen, and the first thing I see is the mess of powdered pancake mix all over the counter and the charred remains of burned batter smokin' away on my plugged-in waffle maker. I rush to it and pry it open, waving smoke away from the pitch-black remains inside.

"What in the world? Y'all are gonna burn my house down with all this foolishness!" I sigh at the counter, one cluttered with measurin' cups, syrup bottles, a softened stick of butter, a pile of silverware, and a couple of plates piled on the Formica.

I start toward the fridge and catch a glimpse of a burly figure at the breakfast nook out of the corner of my eye.

"You're cleaning up this mess, Carl." I shake my head. "What's the matter? Why didn't you go catfishin' today?"

When he doesn't respond, I assume he's scrolling on his doggone phone again. Ignorin' me, as usual. He's always on that stupid thing. Never present.

"I said good m—"

My words are cut short by Jolene's deafenin' scream, one I'm sure everyone can hear all the way down in N'awlins proper. I nearly drop the empty coffee pot when I see the source of her horror.

It's *Carl*. Slumped over, face-first into a small mountain of golden waffles. The gruesome wound on the back of his bald head glistens. Blood trails down him into a puddle on the floor with a few messy footprints smudged into it with a diamond-shaped pattern. The large man is still like he's simply fallen asleep and been doused in strawberry syrup like some fraternity prank. But there's no mistakin' it, that eerie, chillin' level of stillness he's exhibiting…

I don't even waste time shakin' him to see if he'll snap out of it like a deep nap. I can just tell…

This guy is deader'n Elvis.

5

Deputy Amos Landry wanders around my property with yellow "DO NOT CROSS" tape spooled on a pencil, tyin' it to the low branches of my magnolia tree. Then, to my air conditionin' unit, my back gate, and the side mirror of my car.

In his quest to set a perimeter, he drops his roll of canary-yellow plastic on the ground just about every ten seconds or so, readjusting his too-loose belt every time he stands. Poor kid has been yo-yo dietin' ever since he graduated high school. About five minutes ago, I nearly saw him poke his own eye out on a branch from the tree. I don't think he's officially *touched in the head*, but he sure is doggone close, bless his heart. He's surprisingly managed to evade the laws of Darwinism for four whole decades.

Inside my kitchen window, I see Sheriff Moses Cheramie place his balled fists on his wide hips and slouch in a way that shoves his paunch straight out in front of him. He gawks at the corpse of my former future son-in-law, circling the slumped body, studying a horrible sight that I can never unsee.

A few minutes go by, and I feel a firm hand on my shoulder and hear the honey-sweet sound of Cosmo's voice.

"Uma, what's goin' on? Everything alright? Somethin' happen with Jolene or the baby?"

"No," I say, wanting to throw myself against his hardened chest for comfort but finding myself strangely unable to move.

"It… it's Carl. He's dead."

Cosmo gasps, and his hand slinks off my shoulder. Suddenly, my conversation with him last night pops back into my jumbled mind, and I remember that I said some things about *wishing Carl was gone* and *voodoo dolls…* and poking that thing with a needle right in the *head.* Now, the same man is cold as a snow cone and turning stiff at my breakfast nook with a mortal wound in that very spot.

"It wasn't me," I whisper.

"What?" Cosmo seems very confused.

"I said it wasn't me. I didn't kill him."

"I… I didn't suspect ya did." Cosmo looks around and then lowers his head toward me further. "What was he killed with?"

"Well, it wasn't *voodoo*! I can tell you that much!"

Cosmo pinches his ice-blue eyes shut tight in frustration, "I *know*, I meant, what kind of weapon? Was he shot?"

"No, it definitely didn't look like a bullet hole. Way too big and messy for that."

"Could it have been... suicide, maybe? Guy's been under a lot of pressure with the weddin'."

"Let me ask," I say, waltzing right up to the tape line and then a step further still, bowing the tape around my belly like a hideous yellow belt. "Cheramie!"

Cosmo tries to pull me back. "Leave him alone, Uma!"

I shrug his hand off. "Moses Cheramie, boy, you had betta' answer me!"

Moses comes to my kitchen window, watching the floor so that he doesn't destroy evidence. "What, Uma? What is so important? I'm in the middle of somethin' here!"

"It wasn't *suicide*, was it?" I shout, realizing that the squad cars and tape are starting to draw more of a crowd than just Cosmo. I see both of my sisters creepin' up the canopied sidewalk from down the block. Matt and Belinda gawk in pajamas from their flamingo-strewn lawn.

"Uma, pipe down and let me do this investigation!" Moses shakes his head, wide Creole features partly obscured by my thin window sheers. "Just... lemme be, *please*. I'm tryin' to think here!"

I see Amos Landry toss the roll of tape in the trunk of his squad car and open the rear side door. My youngest daughter's wails fill the breeze-less air in this once-quiet neighborhood. This prompts Payzlee to cry. I walk over and hold my hands out for the baby. Jolene hands her over, and through incoherent sobs, she starts blubbering to Amos. He scribbles on a little notepad in handwritin' so messy I don't think he'll ever be able to decipher it once he gets back to the station.

"...And he... we walked in... and there he was... just face-down in his waffles with... with that gapin' wound in his head." She sobs again and screams, "We were about to be married!"

"I see. When was the wedding date, Ms. Blanchard?"

"Saturday! We were gonna get hitched at the church and then have a little shindig down at the Killjoy Rec Center. It wasn't gonna be anythin' real fancy. We didn't have a lotta money because we got this baby on the way."

My mind drifts to my thwarted cruise, the never-endin' mojitos I will never drink, the *Takin' Care of Business* I will never get a standing ovation at karaoke for. My thoughts wander further still to the rigor mortis in Carl's stiffened arms, the aimless compass on his neck hoverin' above the table where I eat my meals, head slumped on a plate of syrupy waffles like a man bowing in deep prayer. I think about the rivulets of red runnin' down the side of the table, pooling on my wooden floorboards. I'm gonna have to bleach that out somehow. Maybe I can have Daniel show me how to pull up some videos on bloodstain removal on that *HueTube* app the twins were telling me about the last time I was over.

Out of the corner of my eye, I see Jacoby standing there, hands stuffed in his pockets, shoulders shrugged up by his ears, exhibiting a sad strength. Poor kid just lost his father, and he's trying to stay strong for Jolene. Didn't seem like his daddy wanted anything to do with him half the time, so maybe this is just another day of disappointment. I'm sure he's had *many* of those in the last nineteen years of being Carl's boy.

"Looks like Carl's got a cell phone in there on the table. We'd like to do a forensic analysis of it and look at the text messages and such. Do you happen to know the code to unlock it, Ms. Blanchard? It would save us a heap'a time tryin' to get the lab boys to crack it."

"Why would I know the code?" I ask, scrunchin' my face.

"Not *you,* Uma!" Amos says. "*Jolene.*"

"Oh…" Jolene says in a trance, staring through the grate separatin' the front seat from the back. She's pickin' at some of the chipped enamel on it. "I think… it's… um… 1-2-1-9-0-6."

Amos jots it in his notepad and circles it. Jacoby's sad eyes flash to me for a moment, and then his gaze returns to the overgrown grass at his feet.

"Is there anyone that you can think of that would have wanted to hurt Mr. Easterly?" Amos asks my daughter. "There anyone he had bad blood with?"

I scoff. That's one heck of a list right there, it seems, judging by last night's little display.

"There were a few people that weren't a fan of him, I guess you could say," Jolene mumbles.

"I need all of their names, Miss."

I interject, bobbing Payzlee's limp body on my hip. She lays her head on my shoulder and rubs her face hard against the material. I nod toward Jolene. "Baby, tell Landry here about Carl's little *visitor* last night."

Jolene looks embarrassed. As if I shouldn't have brought up the most *likely* person who would have ended her fiancee's life. She looks as if the shame of admittin' her man's flaws might be worse than getting no justice at all for such a heinous crime.

"Last night, one of Carl's best friends came to the house."

"At what time?" Amos inquires.

"Ten thirty-eight," I butt in again. "I remember 'cause I looked at the clock." Amos's attention shifts back to me. "Sorry, go on, officer."

"Well, it was his best friend, Cliff."

"Does Cliff have a last name?"

She thinks for a long moment and wipes a tear from her eye. "Owens, I think. Clifford Owens. He works with

Carl at the refinery. They used to be on the same shift together."

"And what did Mr. Owens say or do when he arrived at the house?"

Jolene recants the argument as much as she possibly can. I lean in to fill in the blanks, and Amos keeps trying to swat me away like an obnoxious mosquito hovering 'round his eyeball.

Once she stops talking, I add, "Last night, before bed, Carl had my dinner draped across his black eye. Surely, this has to be the guy you're looking for. Now you have a name. Go bring this man in. Jolene just handed him to you on a silver platter."

"Not so fast, Uma. You should know better'n anyone, what with Harold bein' on the force and all, that this here's a process," Moses booms, walkin' down my cracked pavers and leanin' his arm against my wide-mouth bass mailbox -- *it's the cutest thing, too. Its bottom jaw is the door, and he just gobbles up all that doggone junk mail like it's nothing.*

"A man comes to give the boy a shiner at my house, claimin' that his newborn baby might not even be *his,* and Carl ends up dead the next morning? I'd say that's a pretty open-and-shut case if you ask me."

"Well, I *didn't* ask, as a matter of fact," Moses says curtly, clearly annoyed at my conclusion. "Carl's got a bit of a reputation around these parts."

"Who told you that? Clara?" I ask, referring to the sweet woman with the gigantic yapper who works the front desk at the Sheriff's Department here in Killjoy.

"Clara's got her finger on the pulse of this community, Uma."

"That's because she's out there at the bars and the bowling alleys in everyone's business every night. Woman needs a *hobby*, Moses."

"Well, Clara seems to think Carl's left a whole lotta ticked-off people in his wake since he moved here from Saint Amant."

Moses glances at the back of the squad car where Jolene is sittin' with a face like she just caught a whiff of Bourbon Street -- *which, if you've never smelled it, reeks like sun-dried sick and toxic tinkle… only mixed with the cloyin' scent of high-proof booze and sugar.*

"In a bit, we got the coroner coming. Amos, when he gets here, get him in booties and send him in. I need a T.O.D. stat."

"Is it still Wells Anderson?" I ask, hopeful.

Moses studies me for a long time, chocolate-brown eyes torchin' a hole right through me. "Yes. Why. You *know* him?"

"Son, I know half this *parish*. Wells and I went to school together a long time ago. Heck, we even dated for a stretch." My eyes flash to Jolene, and I add defensively, "Don't worry. It was long before I ever met your daddy."

Jolene shivers involuntarily, most likely at the thought of her aging mother havin' a romantic life.

"Pfft. Yeah. *Looooong* time ago." Moses just *has* to get a dig in about my age. "Back when Killjoy was just a piece of the French Colonial *Empire*…"

"Yeah, because you're some kind of spring chicken *yourself*," I sass back. "I'll bet you're already at the age where you gotta get a prostate exam every year."

Moses turns, fumin' a little, presumably at the truth of the statement. He looks at the window to my kitchen, rubbin' his hands against a belly big enough to rest a bottle of cold Abita on it without spilling. His jacket *whooshes* as he runs his hands against the sweat on the side of his forehead. I remember when he was just a boy, the same age as my son, Daniel. Now Moses is a man, tufts of gray splashed through his kinky temple hair.

Moses leans in toward my ear and speaks lower so that Jolene doesn't hear it. "*I don't see a weapon on the floor or the table. If there isn't one underneath the body when Wells moves him, we can rule out suicide.*"

I growl-whisper back to him, "*The wound is on the back of his head, Moses. I imagine you coulda safely ruled that out already.*"

"Well, if he didn't do it to himself, I'm sorry, Uma, but we can't let you folks back in the house while we got ourselves an active crime scene."

I groan, and Moses takes two steps away from me again. He addresses all of us. "That means that during the duration of our investigation, you will all need to stay somewhere else, ya hear?"

"I can't believe this! You're kicking me out of my own home?"

"Afraid so, Uma."

"Well, ain't *that* a fine how do you do?" I scoff again. "I'm supposed to board a cruise in a few days, and now I gotta deal with all this?"

Moses shakes his head. "No cruise. I'm still going to need to have you each come down and submit an official statement on the record so I can start checking alibis and gettin' to the bottom of this. I need you reachable in case we have any questions."

I stomp my slippered foot petulantly in the grass and shake my citrus-patterned robe at him. "I'm still in my pajamas, for Pete's sake! I can't just go walkin' around Killjoy like this. What'll people think?"

"Sorry, Uma. That's just the way it is," Moses says, shakin' his head.

"Fine. When can I go in and pack an overnight bag?"

"You can't. As of right now, anything in there could be evidence in our investigation. I can't let you back inside."

"Wait, what? I was in my bedroom when all this nonsense happened. Why am I bein' punished?"

"Nonsense? My husband is dead!" Jolene howls. Payzlee follows suit and starts to whine, too.

"*Fiancee*. He wasn't your hubby *yet*, thank goodness!" I say, regrettin' the insensitive words as soon as they leave my mouth. "I'm sorry…"

"Uma," Moses is losin' his patience with me. "Harold was on the force for how long? You know this is simply protocol."

"*Harold* was on the force. Not me. How the heck am I supposed to have all your silly little rules memorized?"

"You can't stay here. Why don't you go crash with one of those cluckin'-hens?" Moses points to Cindy and Liv, my twin sisters, older than me by two years. They're both at the edge of my lawn, pressed against the tape, waving excitedly at Sheriff Cheramie like he's on the red carpet for a movie premiere.

"I'd rather sleep in a homeless shelter." I roll my eyes.

"The baby and I'll stay with Aunt Cindy," Jolene says firmly. "I don't like the idea of Payzlee being cooped up anywhere near Cocodrie. He could probably fit her whole hand in that shark-like little yap of his."

As if he could hear her -- as if he could hear *anything* at his age -- Cocodrie starts to yip, his angry voice muffled by the wooden privacy fence dividing the front and back yards.

"Yeah. That's a good idea. Stay with Cindy. She's used to plannin' funerals anyway. She'll plan Carl somethin' lovely, I'm sure. Like she did with that homeless fella that she found under the bridge last year. The one she called 'her little project' before he promptly kicked the bucket in her bathtub. Boy, what a nice funeral that was."

I mean it. Cindy outdid herself with that one. Bankrolled it with some of the life insurance she's got sitting around from her second dead husband.

I look back at my sisters, fake a smile, and wave to let them know I see them and to stop swinging their hands around like beauty queens.

"Plus," I say, turning back to my youngest, "Cindy's like one of them black widows, so no one would know how to comfort you better. She's lost several men over the years."

Moses finds no humor in my insinuation. Jolene starts to cry again. I reach out to try to stroke her hair, and she pulls away.

"If it's any consolation, Jolene, she's getting real good at the arrangements by now. She knows all the steps and has surprisingly good taste in headstones and service decor. She really ought to do it part-time, honestly."

But my comment doesn't ease Jolene's tears one bit. I've never been good at consolin' people. I'm more of a *rub some dirt in the wound and keep walking* kinda woman.

I sigh, thinkin' about how I don't have a lot of choices for where to stay. Cindy and Liv are gonna have their hands full with a sobbing pregnant woman and a cryin' baby. Cosmo sold his guest bed to make room for a new billiard table. Turned the whole thing into a rec room after his youngest moved out.

For a split second, I even look at the Guidry's house with a glimmer of hope, thinking maybe they could put me up in a spare room on a futon or something. But, I feel a phantom pain shoot up my spine at the thought of it, and I catch another glimpse of that ghastly flock of hot-pink flamingos in their yard, and the thought vanishes like flatulence in the wind.

"I'll figure somethin' out," I say as Cocodrie starts another yappin' fit at the back gate, probably smellin' blood through the open window and rememberin' how he's developed a taste for it as he's gotten old and cranky.

Jacoby pipes up. "Hey, Gran-Gran?"

I grit my molars and try to fight the urge to battle against that doubly terrible nickname, but then I remember that the poor boy just lost his father today. He's been through enough without my piling anything further on top of him.

"*Yes*, Jacoby?" My eyebrows hoist almost to my hairline, trying to express my level of annoyance while still bein' at least a *little* kind to the poor sap.

"Well, I think Dad has an extra room in our family's block at the hotel. You could stay there."

Jolene's face sours almost more than my own. "What?"

I am just as confused. "What do you mean he's got an extra room?"

"Well, I guess he rented four of them, but he only needed three. One for Grandpa and his wife, one for me, and one for Grandma."

"Why didn't he just tell the people at the front he didn't need the extra room?" Moses asks, seemin' just as curious as I am.

"Yeah, we didn't even have enough money to get the real roses I wanted for the bouquets, yet, somehow, he had a few hundred bucks to throw away on an empty hotel room?" Jolene is starting to fume.

It's about time.

Jacoby shrugs hard, looking like he just betrayed his dead Dad's confidence somehow. He reaches out for the baby, and I hand her over. Payzlee latches onto him and buries her face into his neck.

"Originally, it was for my uncle, I think, but I guess he couldn't make it to the wedding. Dad made a joke about just keeping it and using it for the bachelor party."

"Bachelor party?" Jolene winces. "I told him he wasn't havin' one. We were gonna do a Jack-and-Jill type thing together in The French Quarter." She groans and balls her fist like she wants to punch something.

Moses watches with suspicion. I can see him take a mental note of it. The thought of him settin' his sights on her as a potential suspect burns me up. Cops typically look at the spouse or the partner harder'n anyone.

But Jolene was always a peaceful child, slow to anger. She couldn't have done this.

"Okay then, I'll stay at the hotel. Do you know what room, kid? The one that's unoccupied?"

"It's room 307 at the Lagniappe Inn. I can drive you over later if you want."

"That's alright. I know where it's at. I can take the Buick."

Amos laughs. "They ain't taken your license away yet?"

He laughs, and I rear up like I'm gonna give him a whack on the back of his idiot head.

"Might I remind you of the penalty of assaulting an officer, Ms. Blanchard," Moses says, crackin' a slight smile. "I know you need a place to stay. Just 'cause that holdin' cell down at my office is brand new, don't mean it's *comfy*, I assure you."

I put my hand down, pursing my lips to hold in a torrent of curse words I wanna utter.

"Moses, can I talk to you in private over there for a minute?" I say, motioning to the patch of tall grass by where my sisters are still waving like they're watchin' A-list celebrities. Behind them, a fella I don't recognize smoothes his hair in the side mirror of the Channel 8 news van. A few feet away, his cameraman assembles a heavy-looking shoulder rig.

"Yes, Ms. Blanchard?" Moses says with a dubious look on his face like he already knows foolishness is gonna come out of my mouth.

"Moses, you and Harold worked together on the force for a long time. No?"

"Sure." He sighs heavily. I can almost hear the years of fried food taking a toll on his flabby heart. "He trained me when I was greener'n Amos over there."

"So you know I'm trustworthy, right?"

"Uma, you're not going on a cruise until I clear you officially, and it's hard to do that when your alibi is just 'I was asleep,' and no one can account for your whereabouts."

"*Moses Allan Cheramie*, you know I'm not a murderer. If I'd have wanted Carl dead, I'd have strangled him in his sleep the night my precious baby girl came home *engaged* to that creep! Clara ain't the only woman in town who has her ear to the ground. I know this guy was a real…" I lean in closer, like it's a secret, "*Jezebel*."

"Jezebel? I think that's strictly a feminine term, Uma."

"Well, whatever the male version is, then. The boy was a harlot."

"Still feminine."

"Ugh!" I growl in frustration. "Fine. What if I help?"

"Help what?"

"You know, with the investigation. You keep me in the loop on everything, and in exchange, I help you wrap this thing up 'fore noon Saturday. Together, we can put a nice, tidy bow on it so you can go back to crammin' beignets in your mouth, and I can enjoy my five days on the open sea aboard the *Oshannic Aspire*. Whaddaya say?"

"You know darn well I can't divulge information in an ongoin' investigation with a person of interest."

"I'm not a person of interest. I was passed out cold in an *Ambien* slumber. I can give you a list of references that'll vouch I sleep like the dead. So, now that you've downgraded me from a person of interest, you can, instead, think of me sorta like… a private *contractor* of sorts. I'll go out. Do a little diggin'. And in return—"

"Yeah, yeah. Cruise ship. I get it." He waves me off. "Uma, dream on. You're not trained for this. You're involved with the victim *and* our other persons of interest…"

"You know how many cases I helped Harry with over the years in private? I may not know your silly *procedures* well, but I'll tell ya, I solved my fair share of stuff like this from the wings."

"Oh yeah, like what?"

"Remember when all those people were gettin' sick at the elementary school in Edgard 'bout ten years back?"

"*Yeah…*" His eyes light up with suspicion.

"Remember they found that dead horse just rottin' away in the potable water source?"

"*Yeeeeeahhhhh.*" His eyes widen. "Did you… put the horse in there, Uma? Because if you did—"

"No! Moses, use your head. Don't be a dunce. Who do you think figured out that stuff about the horse? Harry thought somethin' was fishy about it, *no pun intended*, and I went on down there in a snorkel and a swimsuit. The dang thing scared me so much I almost soiled the water myself if you catch my drift."

Moses makes a disgusted face. "Yeah, I get it."

"Those little kids were *drinking* that, Cheramie."

"I said *I got it*."

"And what about that guy that knocked over all them banks right there in Garyville and LaPlace? Hmmm? Who do you think helped Harold make that *miraculous arrest* so quick? I pumped the catty women in my book club, scrubbed through hours of security footage from the businesses next door, and ended up leading y'all right there to his beat-up Chevy in that little run-down fish and chips joint in Belle Point."

"You can do anything you want, Uma. I can't stop you. But you're sure as hell not helping my office in any *official* or *unofficial* capacity."

"Okay," I wink. "I get it. Everything's off the record."

"There is no *record*. I've got this handled, Ms. Blanchard."

"Okay." I smile and exaggerate another wink. "*Got it*."

"I don't think you do." Moses shakes his head. Just as he does, another white van pulls up, one similar to the news van without the gaudy signage. In tasteful letters on the side, it simply says CORONER in a block font. The second the engine sputters and dies, Wells Anderson hops out like a spry little elf, all bones and blue jeans, baggy T-shirt billowing on his wiry frame. I can see his wide smile beam all the way from the street, peeking out beneath his curled white mustache, one that makes him look like Rip Torn went on a Gandhi-style hunger strike.

"Well," he shouts to Moses, too peppy for such a somber occasion, "how 'bout all this sunshine lately? I swear, I'm gon' need to bump up my SPF down at the house. I've been gettin' fried just drinkin' beer on my dock."

He throws a satchel of jinglin' tools over his shoulder and flashes a dirty smile at my twin sisters. "*Ladies.*"

"Oh, my, Mr. Anderson, have you been working out?" Cindy says flirtatiously, even though it looks like a little set of runner's hand weights might weigh more than Wells himself.

"Wellsy, I ain't seen you in a *minute*," Cindy shouts, lookin' like she wants to eat him for dinner.

"You ladies should come on down to *The Flytrap* sometime and buy me a beer," he says in the thickest southern accent known to man, wigglin' his butt playfully at them. "Buy me a few, and I might just let you get a little frisky with me."

Cindy blushes.

"Dream on, Wellsy," Liv hollers, arms folded, face turned away in protest. Then, she punctuates the whole scene with a scoff. Cindy swats at her for bein' rude.

"Well, Liv, if you wise up one day and decide you wanna take a walk on the wild side, you know where to find me. My number ain't changed in decades, doll."

Wells winks at my sisters and ducks under the tape. He strolls casually across the lawn, sets his bucket of supplies down, and wraps his skeletal arms around me. He squeezes with a strength he doesn't look like he should physically have bein' a five-foot-nothing waif. Probably only a buck-even when he's soakin' wet. A stiff wind could blow his bony butt right down the block.

"Uma Mae Blanchard, I don't think I've seen that pretty face of yours since Harold's funeral."

"Has it been that long?"

I start to do the math in my head, but Moses grabs Wells's scrawny shoulders and guides him toward my house, perturbed. "As fun as this little reunion is, we have a body decomposing inside that I'd really like a time-a-death on as soon as possible."

"Of course," Wells says with a nod.

"Way to make it weird, Moses." I shake my head.

Wells digs in a section of his bag marked 'PPE' and pulls out a set of blue rubber gloves and some elastic booties. He slides the gloves on with a stingin' smack as he and the Sheriff make their way to my front door.

Moses looks back over his shoulder at me. "Stay local, Uma. Don't do anything foolish. I promise I'mma get whoever done this to your son. You've got my word on that."

"He wasn't my *son*," I holler across the lawn just before I catch my youngest child mean-mugging me for the comment from the back of Landry's squad car.

"Thanks, Ma," she huffs.

6

Cindy puts a cup of tea down in front of me, and I wince.

"Don't you have anything stronger? Like coffee? For God's sake, a man just *died*." I push the cup away.

"You know where the instant grounds are, Uma." Cindy points at the kitchen.

"I'd rather eat Cocodrie's kibble than drink that trash. Is this at least high-caf?"

Cindy shakes her head. "Decaf. Ginger and turmeric. It's good for gut health. Plus, tea is chock-a-block full 'a antioxidants."

"I don't need antioxidants. I need *caffeine*. I had people bangin' on my door all night, and I woke up to a body."

"Well, you are just all kinds of fussy today, aren't you?" Cindy shakes her head.

"Moses is makin' me cancel my cruise!"

"Oh, *poor baby*," she mocks. "Uma, your son-in-law just passed. Show some respect."

I sigh and look out her window at the circus on my lawn half a block down. Yellow crime scene tape twists in place around the perimeter, and I see Moses writing out notes on a little pad using the trunk of my Buick as his makeshift clipboard.

The news anchor is in the middle of some sort of news report about it, blathering on as the cameraman follows him along the sidewalk. Suddenly, I feel self-conscious about the length of my lawn. I should've given Jacoby a couple of bucks to mow it yesterday. Heck, I'll bet Landry's stomping all over my hostas, too!

Liv walks in and sighs, running a hand through her stark-white hair. It lost all its color a good two decades before her fraternal twin and me. "Payzlee finally went down. Poor thing was all wound up from that commotion over there."

Cindy nods, always the calmer of the twins. "What's Jolene doin'?"

"Oh, she done cried herself to sleep a half an hour ago. She's in the chaise next to the crib, passed out cold."

"You sure it's okay if she stays here?" I ask.

"Oh, of *course*. Don't be silly. We'd love the company. Plus, I know how much you can't stand a screamin' baby," Cindy says, almost singin' it like a bird.

"If I'm gonna be stayin' in some rinky-dink motel room, I just can't have Jolene whippin' out her flapjacks to pump for Payzlee every time I turn around. I mean, I know I seen her naked as a child, but it feels… just… I dunno… *icky* as an adult."

Liv laughs.

"What?"

"Oh, nothin'. Just my almost-seventy-year-old little sister usin' the word icky like she's in grade school. You still afraid of cooties, too?" Cindy asks with a chuckle.

"Excuse me for not having a better vocabulary," I grumble, toying with the handle of my teacup.

"You know, I overheard the Sheriff sayin' to Amos that the back door to the house was wide open this mornin' when he came in. Y'all really should lock up around here. That whole safe, small-town thing is an outdated myth," Liv warns, taking a sip of her own drink.

I furrow my white brows. "Wait. That *can't* be. Jolene always locks the doors at night. She's real paranoid about that stuff now that she had Payzlee."

"Well, who opened it then?" Cindy asks.

Liv gasps, "Oh, holy Moses, maybe it's a clue! Maybe it's like... you know, the killer came from inside the home!"

"You watch too many movies, Liv." I roll my eyes and finally take a sip of the tea, grimacing. "Ugh, there isn't even anything *in* this. No sugar or milk. Nothing."

"You know where the kitchen is," Liv says without looking at me. "You also know where the front *door* is."

"Pfft. Y'all are *real* welcoming today." I shake my head.

Cindy retreats to the kitchen for a moment, clanging around in the cupboards.

Liv ignores my comment. "Tea is good for you anyway. It's full of—"

"*Antioxidants*. Yeah, I know. I heard. And this one moves your bowels or something." I push it away from me. That's gonna be a hard pass.

My oldest sister -- older'n Liv by two minutes, a fact that helped us navigate through many impasses growing up as siblings -- returns from the kitchen with a medium-sized moving box in her arms. She plops it on the table near me, rattling my saucer.

"What's this?"

"Made you a little care package. You know, snacks and essentials. Who knows how long you're gonna be holed up at that fleabag motel."

Liv chimes in. "It's mostly just hot sauce and spices and things. I'm sure the food around that hotel'll be bland."

I smile. As much as they were the bane of my existence growing up, they've become real nurturing as they've aged. I'm still waiting for that attribute to really tickle my fancy. So far, it hasn't. "Thanks."

I rifle through the box. It's full of crackers, clipped bags of chips, half a jar of peanut butter, an unopened jar of jelly, half a loaf of bread, and some Cajun seasonings. "Thank you for this. That's real nice."

Liv and Cindy nod in unison. Almost feels like they share a brain sometimes.

I stand and grab the box of food. "I'm gonna head over to the hotel and see if I can get in that room. I'd like to watch this craziness on the news and see if I can get any updates or clues. Plus, I gotta call and see if I can get a refund on my cruise."

"Where were you going this time?" Liv asks.

"Cozumel and the Yucatan."

"Mmmmm. Remember those tacos we had outside that cave in the Yucatan? The place where they had the *horchata*?" Cindy asks.

My smile turns into a frown. "Sure do."

"Awww. Poor baby." Liv breezes over and rubs my back. "You'll cruise again soon. I'm sure of it." I feel her comforting hand start to subtly push me toward the door, almost as if she is trying to kick me out subconsciously. I take the hint and walk toward it on my own.

"Thanks for the snacks," I say, hoisting the box up with gratitude.

"Don't mention it," Liv says.

"Don't worry, I won't."

Cindy doesn't laugh. "If you need anything, call. In the meantime, we'll hold down the fort with Jolene and the baby."

"Do me a favor," I say, eyeing both of them seriously. "If you see anything out of the ordinary there at my house, you call me."

"Will do."

Liv opens the door for me, and I step out onto their porch. It is full of potted gardenias and budding rose bushes. Seems Daddy gave us girls all his green thumb.

I look at her doorbell. It's one'a them fancy ones with a camera built in. "Liv, does this thing record?"

"Yeah, but it's on a motion detector, and it keeps recording the cloud cover and every car that drives through. I doubt it would have anything from last night. I keep meanin' to have Cosmo come change the settings."

A twinge of jealousy tightens in my gut at the thought of my sisters flirting with the most handsome, eligible senior bachelor in a three-block radius. I should know. I've done some fairly intense scouting on my walks with Cocodrie.

"Why Cosmo? Why not the tech boys that installed it?"

"Oh, I don't want to make an appointment to futz with all that nonsense. He has the same one. Cosmo's tech-savvy, you know. Heck, he even taught me how to use my email a while back."

I wanna tell her to stay away from my eye candy, but she's given me an idea. "Cosmo has the same one?"

"Oh, yes, he loves it. He was talking it up at a crawfish boil one day. It's why Cindy and I decided to get one in the first place. You never can be too careful these days." She points to the gaggle of people gathered at the yellow tape line on my lawn. "Case in point."

"You're not wrong there, Liv." I step off the curb, deep in thought. "Catch you later."

7

Cosmo's doorbell chimes. His spaniel howls, muffled by the door.

Nothing.

Ding-dong.

I ring again, hunching down to peer straight into the wide-angled lens pointed right at the gawking podcasters and newsmen tramplin' my Bermudagrass.

"Howdy, neighbor," a voice finally says, only it is twenty feet to my left. It startles me, and I nearly drop my box of food right there on the concrete. Peekin' above the wooden privacy fence, I see the streaked tufts of gray-and-black hair swooped into an effortless wave above that devilishly handsome set of blue eyes, ones that pierce straight through me in my fondest dreams.

"Lord, Cosmo, you scared the daylights out of me! Why can't you come to the front door like a normal person?"

"I was out back doin' my sun salutations, about to light up a stogie. You want one?" He cracks the gate open for me, and I can see that he's shirtless again. *Thank the Lord above.* While it may be a common sight, it's one that never fails to take my breath away.

"No, thanks. You got a cup of coffee, though? I'm jonesin' hard for some quality java, and I got a couple questions for ya. Won't take but a moment of ya time."

"Don't be silly! Come on back to the grotto. I'll fire up the Keurig."

"Oh, you truly are a Saint." I shuffle into his backyard, and he latches the gate closed behind me, brushing against me with a strong arm.

"Saint Goodman," he says with a chuckle. "Doesn't have a bad ring to it." He looks at the box as I set it down by the small bistro table. "What's all that? You movin'?"

"Jus' temporarily. Cindy and Liv made me take it. They said the food down by the dump where I'm staying during all this chaos is sub-par."

"Where you stayin'?" He heads through the wide-open sliding glass door to a small rack with a coffee maker on it just inside.

"Lagniappe Hotel."

"Ew," Cosmo says reflexively.

"Yeah, I know. Apparently, Carl had been keepin' an extra room there. An empty one."

"Weird. I didn't know he had that kind of money."

"He didn't," I say, eyeing the massive beds of zinnias on either side of Cosmo's rock waterfall. He built it by hand four summers ago. The pumps for it filter the koi pond at the bottom. It's stocked with massive orange-and-white goldfish-lookin' things all swimmin' around contentedly. It's quite peaceful to look at, actually.

In front of the landscaped grotto is a patch 'a grass with a foldin' chair on it. A glass of iced lemonade sweats on the front flap of the espionage thriller paperback on the ground beside it. Cosmo must've been getting' a tan. On either side of the mat are thick bunchings of palm trees and tropical foliage. It's like a tiny island paradise right here in his backyard.

"I thought the extra expense was curious myself. Carl had to borrow money from me just to afford the venue," I add. "So, the fact that he's bein'... sorry... he *was* being so frivolous with money kinda irks me."

Cosmo pops his head out the door. "I'd be real mad, too, Uma. Only met the guy a couple of times, but I could tell he was a few crayons shy of a full box."

I cop a squat in one of the shaded chairs beneath the bistro table's large collapsible umbrella. I prop my feet up in another chair and make myself at home, listenin' to the soft rush of water as it dribbles down the rock face.

"Black, right?" he asks.

I nod. "Yup. No frills."

"Psychopath." Cosmo shakes his head and smiles, bringin' me out a steamin' cup of Joe. He sets it on the tabletop in front of me.

"Thank ya kindly, Cosmo." I pick it up by the handle and look at the stylized logo on the side. It feels familiar.

"Wrap party gift for an action flick I did back in '08."

"What'd you do in that one?" I ask, blowing on the steamin' contents, anxious to get it in me sooner rather than later.

"Well, let's see. I took a punch in a nightclub scene and flew over the bar, smashed a *buncha* glass."

I chuckle, watching the coffee nearly lap over the top of the mug onto me.

"Then, in another scene, there was a car chase. I was one of the drivers for that. And then there's a part where the lead hits a pedestrian…"

"Let me guess… *you* were that pedestrian?"

"Guilty as charged. They had to hit me with that sedan *four* times to get the take. Darn near broke another rib."

A shiver goes through me despite the swelterin' heat descending upon Killjoy. I always get so excited when he talks about his dangerous exploits.

"You have lived a million lives," I say, finally taking a delightful sip of the brew. My eyes flutter.

"Good?"

"Amazin'." I take another sip and then set it down.

"So what'd you wanna ask me?"

"Well, a couple things ain't sitting right with me 'bout Carl's murder."

"Alright." He leans in, intrigued. "Like what?"

"Well, for one thing, word has it, the back door to my house was unlocked. The lock wasn't busted, either. Jolene *always* locks that. I know I didn't kill the man. It surely wasn't Jolene, though I honestly wouldn't blame her if she had. I was barely around the guy, and I wanted to strangle him after the first day or two 'a knowin' him. You're the only other person with a key to that door."

"Woah," he puts his rough hands up defensively and leans back in his chair. "If you're saying that you think *I* had something to do with this—"

"Oh, heavens no! Of course not."

"You gave me that thing so I could watch over your plants and bring in your mail—"

"Oh, honey, I know that. I just... I don't know. The whole thing about the back door just ain't sitting right. I can't imagine him or Jolene gave a copy of my key to anyone."

I take a longer swig of the coffee and smack my lips, feelin' the caffeine course through my thin veins.

"Also," I don't quite know how to broach the subject, so I just blurt it plainly, "I told the Sheriff I'm gon' try to help him find who did this. Mostly for selfish reasons, you see."

"The cruise?" He chuckles.

I nod, embarrassed over seeming so petty.

"Any way I can help?" He smiles, and his blue eyes twinkle, even in the hot shade.

"Yeah, actually. That camera on your doorbell. Does it record?"

"Yeah, it does. Pretty decent quality, too. In the daylight, that is. At night, it's hit-and-miss."

"You think you could make me a copy of that footage 'fore you hand it over to Cheramie?"

He hesitates. "Yeah, probably. I could email you the files."

"I'll take Jacoby to the store to help me pick out a laptop since I can't go in my house. Probably do him some good to get his mind off all this mess."

"Shouldn't be a problem. You still got the same email address?" He laughs. "The 'youaintseennothinyet' Yahoo one?"

"Of course. BTO, baby." I smile.

"Anything else?"

"Yeah, I know you got the spares to my house. Did I give you one for the Buick, too?"

He laughs hard. "Yeah, actually, you did. You gave me the valet key 'cause you locked yourself out of it at the grocery store last fall, and I had to come slim-Jim your car to get it open."

"Oh yeah."

"I believe after I got you in, you then promptly backed into the cart return and mangled it up like a twisty straw."

My face reddens. "Oh yeah. I seem to remember that, too."

"I'm professionally *trained* for collisions, and I still genuinely fear you on the road, Uma."

"*Anyway*," I say, anxious to change the subject. "My keys are in the house, and they won't let me go in. I'd like to have my wheels, so I was wondering if I could get that spare set from you."

"Sure, no problem."

"One last request 'fore I go."

"Anything, beautiful."

The words stop my heart like a stroke, and I have to flex my fists to make sure that's not what's *actually* happening. "I… uh… I was wonderin' if you had a leash and a couple extra dog bowls I could borrow for Cocodrie."

"You want me to just watch him while you're at the hotel?"

"Nah, I could use the company. Maybe havin' him there will scare away any ballsy rodents that feel like they want to test my patience."

Cosmo laughs again. He leaves the table, and by the time I finish my coffee, he returns with a canvas tote full of dog kibble, bowls, and other pet supplies. I rise to take it, and he places the keys in my hand, fingers grazing my palm slowly as he releases the ring. I feel like my knobby knees might buckle.

"Call me if you need anything. I'll get that footage sent over as soon as I can. Have Jacoby show you how to unzip files once you get set up."

I laugh, thinkin' he's makin' a joke. As if one could *unzip* a digital document like a pair 'a pants. Soon, I realize he isn't joking, and I nod.

***

Ten minutes later, Cocodrie's on the leash, and I'm barely bleedin'. His bites are gettin' weaker. Either that, or I am becomin' immune to his random acts of punishment. I should've never named him after the Cajun word for "alligator."

It no longer seems cute.

I put him in the passenger seat of the Buick and holler at the grouping of officers having a pow-wow beneath my magnolia tree.

"Hey, you motley gaggle of Barney Fifes, can you get your stupid yellow tape off my mirror? I'd like to leave." I motion to it with my bitten hand, now starting to drip a little, thanks to all my doctor-prescribed blood thinners.

Cocodrie just sneers in the front seat, pleased with himself, probably wishin' he could see the damage with his foggy eyes so he could relish my pain even more.

None of the uniformed men respond. I shrug and slide into the driver's seat slowly. The chihuahua sadist on the passenger side don't take kindly to sudden movements. Ridin' with him feels a little like tryin' to relax in a hot tub with a loose piranha in it.

"They don't wanna take off the tape… I'll take it off *for* them," I mutter to the ancient dog at my side, who has no clue what's going on. He only knows he has a taste of blood and probably wants more.

I turn the key and crank the shifter into reverse, backin' my Buick out swiftly. The tape yanks back with me and snaps at the end of my driveway, ruinin' their silly little perimeter. As I barrel backward, I feel the tap of my bumper. I look in the rear-view. Seems I collided with the news van parked in front of Cosmo's house.

Whoopsie.

I hear the angry "Hey!" of the cameraman as I shift into drive. I pull forward a few feet and eye the damage in my mirror. Maybe it's my eyes, but it looks fine to me. Seems like the man's being a bit of a baby about it. I pump the gas and jolt forward, hoppin' the curb and takin' out a pink flamingo with a loud *thwack*, missing the Guidry's mailbox by a foot as I correct back onto the street.

8

"Yeah, so it says here that the room was rented by a Carl Easterly. You're not on the reservation, so, unfortunately, I can't issue you a card. You'd have to have Carl come in here and request one," the man says. Beneath his scraggly armpit-level blond hair, I can make out the word "EDDIE" on his name tag.

I follow his terracotta-colored eyes down to a spot on my shirt where a glob of roux has made its new home on one of the lime slices on my pajama shirt.

Did I look strange eatin' outside in slippers and pajama pants at the curbside diner on Airline Highway? *Of course.* But not as strange as I look now with food all over my chest. My hair is still a mess, and I haven't showered for the day yet, so I'm certain that, with my attire and the gravy on my shirt, I look like I just escaped a mental asylum.

Then again, looking around at the run-down state of this place, I might still not even be the worst-dressed person here.

"Look, Eddie. That's going to pose a bit of a problem. That ain't possible." I drum my brittle fingernails on the counter and resist the urge to tongue my dentures out, a bad habit I sometimes have when I'm anxious.

I don't want to play my entire hand with this guy. If he finds out that Carl kicked the bucket, I might be outta a room that I, in a roundabout way, already paid for.

"And if you're gonna have a dog in here, there's a non-refundable pet fee and a waiver you gotta sign."

Cocodrie growls as if he knows Eddie's talkin' about him.

"You look familiar, Eddie. Do I know you?" I ask, trying to soften this guy in any way I can think of.

"No, I don't think so." He squints his eyes as if he's trying to place me.

"You got a last name, Eddie?"

"Pickles." The toe-headed man nods and scratches the scruff on his face.

Pickles? Is this kid serious?

"Oh, I think I used to go to church with your mom," I lie.

"I don't rightly see how that's possible, ma'am. My mother never lived in Louisiana." He pronounces it with five syllables instead of three, so I know *he* wasn't born and raised here.

Out of ideas, I smile cordially. "Would you excuse me for a second?"

"Sure." He smiles and goes back to clickin' away at the game of solitaire on his computer.

I walk outside with my demon dog, looking for a place I can go to scream without drawing too much attention.

I walk around the parking lot, eyeing the Pepto-pink and seaweed green color scheme of the three-story hotel. I see room 307 and study the window. The curtains are open. I could *swear* I see movement, a ghostly specter moving inside. I look at

Cocodrie and then eye the three treacherous flights of steep stairs.

"Gran-Gran!" a voice hollers from the pool. I know who it is by the dumb moniker alone.

Jacoby.

He yanks himself up the side of the pool and slaps his wet feet across the concrete toward me, leaving a trail of chlorinated water in his wake. He snatches a pair of rumpled jeans off a lounge chair and wraps the accompanying towel around his neck.

"You made it," he says, voice somber as his eyes cast down to his swim trunks covered in comic-style monkey faces. I can tell he's trying to keep things together, trying to put on a brave face for the family. I'm sure half of the third-floor wing is in full-blown mournin' right now.

"You brought the dog." He tries to force a smile, the same look most people who know Cocodrie give me when they see the creature.

"Yep." That's all I know to say. What I want to say is, at his age, any day could be his last, but I'm pretty sure that's the last thing Jacoby needs to hear right now.

"You get checked in?" He crosses his wet arms across his doughy, pale chest, and I can see that, just like his daddy, he's got random flash art indelibly inked on him. Bet there isn't a story behind a single one of 'em.

"Nope. They said since I'm not on the reservation, only Carl could give me a key."

"I got you." Jacoby takes charge, marching his wet behind right past me and into the office. He steps to the counter, and Eddie Pickles peels his eyes from the computer screen.

"Hi, yes. My mother-in-law needs a key to her suite," Jacoby bluffs. "Ma, could you and Cocodrie go hang out by the pool? I'll only be a minute."

I look down at the dog, confused. Cocodrie just stares out the door, bottom teeth juttin' out over his upper lip like a beige crocodile, stank breath foggin' the glass, eyes squintin' with suspicion at the blurry shapes outside. His pale, apple-shaped head shakes like he's vibratin'.

"Sure." I leave the tiny lobby with reluctance, giving Jacoby the space to do his thing.

Outside, I watch as Jacoby and Eddie speak, occasionally pointin' to me and the dog. Jacoby fishes his wallet out of the pants in his arms and slides something across the countertop to Eddie, presumably the cash for the pet deposit.

They chat for a moment, and Eddie laughs before swipin' two key cards through a machine and handin' 'em over to Jacoby. He waves and exits, draping his jeans over the crook of his arm and handing me a key card.

"Here. You take one, and I'll take the other in case you need me to take the dog for a walk or anything."

"How'd you do that, *cher*?"

He smiles a little. "Guess this is the first time looking like my daddy's worked out in my favor." He scrubs his wet hair with the towel. "We had that cold snap where temperatures dipped at night last week. I remember Dad was wearing a beanie when he checked in. I only remember it because I thought about getting one just like it. Seems our hair was about the only difference between us."

"Don't sell yourself short, kid. In my book, there's a *lot* that's different about you." I fiddle with my key card.

"You got a suitcase you want me to bring up?"

My eyes bolt open. It's the first time, in all the commotion of the day, that I remember that I have a bag stuffed to the gills with cruise clothes in my trunk. I am so happy I could faint. Or maybe it's the heat...

"As a matter of fact, I do."

Less than ten minutes later, I have re-parked my Buick -- at Jacoby's insistence -- off the curb and into the *actual* parking space I had originally been aimin' for. Jacoby lugs my beast of a bag up the stairs while I trail with Cocodrie, who walks like he's trying to skate through three inches of molasses.

"I'll let you get settled in, but if you want to grab some grub later, I could use the distraction." Jacoby shrugs, heading back toward the stairs, no doubt so that he can get back in the pool while the weather's nice.

"I'll tell you what, kid. I'm gonna take a few hours to get myself situated and unpacked. If you help me pick out a laptop this afternoon at the store, dinner's on me. I know a great little po boy place by the office supply store. It's top-notch."

"Sounds good, Gran-Gran."

I don't have the guts to correct him about the fact that we aren't related, that Carl's gone, and now the kid's technically nothin' to me but an acquaintance.

"I'm your neighbor there in 306," he adds, "so just holler when you're ready to go. The walls are thin. I'll hear ya."

He smiles and heads down the stairs. He's a good kid. Definitely must get his personality from his mama.

Cocodrie decides to release his bladder right there in front of 307, and I moan, throwin' my head back. "Oh, come on, dude. Five minutes on the grass and nothin', and now suddenly it's like Niagra Falls?"

Cocodrie peers up in the general direction of my voice, lookin' real darned pleased with himself. I glance up at the cloudless sky and the awning, knowin' Mother Nature ain't gon' rinse it away any time soon.

I swipe my card, and the lock lights up green. I drag my bag inside, drop the leash, and go in search of a plastic-wrapped cup so's I can rinse the piddle.

Instead, I find an ice bucket. That'll do!

I hurry into the bathroom to fill it with water. I do this so fast that I don't even have time to register the balled-up lacy panties at my feet or the bathroom light burning bright. It isn't until I hear the naked woman in the bubble-filled tub scream bloody murder that I realize Cocodrie and I are not alone.

9

"What are you doing in here?!" The woman shouts at the top of her lungs, scramblin' to cover her bosom, sloshin' water sloppily all over the bathroom floor.

"I could ask you the same exact question, Missy!" I say it with confidence, but inside, I'm wonderin' if I mistakenly went into the wrong room. But if that's the case, why'd my key card work?

And why does the door say 307?

"Put on a towel and come out here! I don't need to see all that," I yell, shieldin' my eyes from her, tossing the woman one'a the pathetic terry-cloth scraps 'a fabric that passes for a towel in this roach-infested joint.

Minutes later, the woman emerges from the bathroom, long graying hair wrapped in a damp bun atop her head, towel *barely* coverin' her robust figure. There's an unmistakable look of shame on her face.

Cocodrie is on the queen bed by me, one that's *fortunately* still turned down.

The woman in the towel takes one look at the dog and grimaces like she ate somethin' rancid. "Is that thing… alive or *taxidermied*?"

Cocodrie lets out a half-snarl-half-bark. A blind predator in search of prey.

"Does *that* answer your question?" I ask smugly.

He growls fiercely, ready to attack. *Who*, he doesn't exactly know, but he's decided that *someone… anyone…* is gon' feel his wrath.

She nods, hesitant to step any closer. She stands with her back against the bathroom door jamb, never takin' her eyes off the dog.

"State your name." I say it like an order, the way Harold would have said it to someone during a line of questionin' while his hand hovered over his service weapon.

"Annie."

"You got a last name, Annie?"

"Waghorn." She looks like she wants to cry.

"Annie Waghorn, what *exactly* are you doin' in my room?"

There is a moment of silence, and in it, I realize I am askin' the wrong question entirely. I rephrase it.

"No. Annie, what are you doing in *Carl Easterly's* hotel room?" I study her angrily. "Let me guess. Third cousin thrice removed?"

"I thought I…" She looks away for a moment. "I don't know what to say. It's all going to sound bad."

"How about you stick with the truth? I ain't got time for games."

"I'm… here to see *Carl*."

"It's a little late for that, don't you think?"

She looks at her watch. "I didn't realize it was checkout time. There must've been a mistake. I thought he had the room for a few more days."

"Sure did." I cross my arms, and Cocodrie must sense my frustration 'cause he starts to growl again, only he does so with his face pointed toward a wall three feet to her right because his senses are so poor.

"Are you… *another* one?" she asks, horrified, lookin' me up and down like she's sizin' me up.

"Another one of *what*?"

"Another… like me."

"Annie, I still have no clue *what* you are."

Her face flushes bright red. "Look. I knew he was with someone. I had no clue it was you. This thing with us was just a fling. I don't think it was anything more'n that. Just a really fun time. It didn't *mean* nothin'."

I'm appalled. Less by the fact that she's alludin' to an affair with my would-be son-in-law, more appalled by the fact she thinks *I'd* stoop that *low*. I *have* standards. He may have been twenty-five years younger'n me, but even on my *worst* day, even at sixty-eight, I could do much better'n him.

"I'm not having an affair with Carl. Are you crazy?" I shout. Cocodrie lets out another loud puff of raunchy air as if to agree with me. I waft his rank breath away before I gag.

"Wait." She's confused. "Then who *are* you?"

"I'm his fiancee's *mother*!"

Her knees buckle, and tears fill her eyes. "Oh my God, I think I'm gon' be sick."

"Well, if you are, the ice bucket's right there. Don't do it on the carpet. It's nasty enough without the added help."

"I didn't know Melissa and him were engaged!"

I can hear my old record player scratch across the vinyl ridges of the ELO *Time* album in my head, haltin' everything at once.

"Who in the *world* is Melissa?!"

"Wait, who is your *daughter*?"

"Jolene Blanchard!"

"I think I'm gonna faint!" Annie crumples, catching herself on the bland table behind her and shaking the decrepit coffee pot on it.

"How long've you been seein' Carl?" I ask, feelin' a migraine come on from all this nonsense. I try to picture myself sunnin' on the lido deck of the Aspire to lower my blood pressure.

"A few months. We were fooling around. He said he wasn't in a relationship. Then, one day, I saw some texts buzzin' on one of his phones while he was in the shower gettin' washed up. I snooped. I'm a nosy person."

"What do you mean *phones*? As in... *plural*?"

"Yeah, he said one was his personal one, and the other was his work phone."

"Work phone? I only ever saw him with the one. What'd they look like?"

"One was in a plain black case. One had, like, a Hindu... thing... on the back of it."

"What kinda *Hindu* thing?"

"I don't know. I just think it looked Hindu. It matched a tattoo on the back of his thigh."

I shudder at the thought of anyone havin' to look at the back of that man's naked legs, much less *several* people...

"Anyway, so he's getting all these texts from her, and I'll admit, I got jealous."

That's weird. Jolene always prefers to call. She says people can't understand her inflections over texts. "When you say he was getting' all these texts from *her*... Who is *her*?"

"Melissa." She says it like I'm touched in the head. Like it's obvious. "She was wonderin' where he was at, why he wasn't home. I feel terrible. I knew she existed, and eventually, I even knew she had a baby on the way, but I didn't stop seeing him." She starts to sob. "I'm a terrible person!"

"Well, you ain't gonna win any awards for integrity with *me*," I say coldly, tryin' to connect all these dots in my mind.

She cries harder. Now I feel a little bad. "Oh, it's alright." I don't know why I feel the need to console her, but I do. She's hysterical. "Carl was the one lyin' to begin with."

"I know," she blubbers. "I just… I get so lonely, and he just was so darn charmin'."

I chew my lip for a moment, and Cocodrie curls up into a ball, eyes still narrowed like a sentinel, ready to attack anything and everything at a moment's notice.

"What's Melissa's last name?"

"The phone just said Melissa O."

I search my brain's directory for any last name that starts with an 'O' in Killjoy. Suddenly, it dawns on me that I heard one just a few short hours ago on my front lawn.

Ugh, it's not even dinnertime, and this day has felt like a month.

"Was it *Owens*?"

"I don't know," she sobs.

"Might be Clifford's wife."

"Who's Clifford?"

My mind flashes back to the man screaming on my front lawn last night about the paternity of his newborn. The shock of seein' Carl drowned in his syrup this morning was a heck of a shock, but findin' out there might be a whole *string* of recently-scorned men and women in his wake certainly complicates things.

"Nevermind. Don't worry about it." I stare at her for a moment. "So, let me see if I understand this. Woman-to-woman, be truthful with me, hun. You got jealous that he was having himself a baby with this Melissa woman, so last night, you took matters into your own hands and got your revenge."

"*Revenge?*" She looks shocked, just as I suspected she'd pretend to be at an outright accusation. "What are you *talking* about?"

"In the wee hours of the mornin', you took matters into your own hands, and you got him back for all the pain he caused you. Didn't you? What'd you hit him with? I'm dyin' to know."

"What? *Hit* him? What are you… I don't understand, ma'am."

"The jig is up, Annie Waghorn. I caught you red-handed in my hotel room washin' off all the evidence right there in 'at tub!"

"Evidence? What're you talkin' about? Carl rented me this room so we could… *you know…*"

I look at the sheets I'm sittin' on, and suddenly I feel queasy. I rise and make my way across the threadbare carpet to the rollin' chair near the desk. I sit in it and lean back, feelin' like I'm in one of those TV interrogations now.

"What'd you kill him with, Annie? The cops are gonna want that weapon."

"K-kill?" she stammers. Her eyes flood with fresh tears. "Carl's…?"

"Your boyfriend is worm-chow." I clasp my fingers together on the desk in front of me. "But you already knew *that*."

"Carl's dead?"

I just stare at her. She looks like she's gonna collapse for real this time. The sobbing is harder now, and she starts tryin' to form words, but none are coherent enough to understand.

"Where were you last night? Hmmm? Sittin' here all alone? That's a real flimsy alibi, Ms. Waghorn. Or is it *Mrs.* Waghorn? With Carl, I guess I shouldn't assume."

"It's Miss. I'm single."

"Well, you made sure of *that* when you cracked the man's cranium like a geode."

"I didn't hurt Carl! I would never hurt Carl! We talked about goin' away together, startin' a family!"

I laugh. "Get in the queue, Ms. Waghorn. He already has a *few* of those." I lean forward, click on the wall-mounted lamp, and twist the sconce so that the bulb is under lightin' me like some sort of Kubrick movie villain. "You killed him, and you came back here to get rid of the evidence. Just say it."

"I was at work all night! I just got off my shift. I came to relax and get cleaned up. He was supposed to come and spend the mornin' with me!"

"Told *us* he had plans to go catfishin' today."

"Well, I can't speak to that, Miss..."

"Blanchard. Uma Blanchard. I was that deadbeat's future mother-in-law. He was about to walk down the aisle with my daughter. Got a kid on the way with her, too."

"Oh God." Annie weeps freely again. "Look, Ms. Blanchard, I was at work all night. You can talk to my shift leader at the hospital. There are cameras and on-shift doctors who can all vouch for my whereabouts until about 9 a.m. this morning."

I study her for a moment to see if she's lying, but her eyes look sincere. I grab the hotel's notepad and pen and slam it on the desk in front of her.

She stares down at my age-spotted hand. "What's that for?"

"It's for you to write down your name, number, and address. The sheriff's bound to have a whole slew of questions for ya."

She nods and writes her information down, even volunteerin' the name of her shift leader at the hospital and his number as well.

I stare at the paper for a long time. Then, I finally glance up. "I don't want to be rude, Ms. Waghorn, but I believe we're done here. I'd love it if you'd take your leave."

"Of course." She nods and collects her things, pullin' a set of lacy lingerie outta the bathroom and stuffin' it into a brand-name purse in the ripped corner armchair.

"...And do me a favor, Annie."

"Yes, ma'am?"

"If you're going to be so bold as to attend the man's funeral, please don't speak one word of this to my daughter, Jolene. She's goin' through enough right now. I'd like to shield her from as much unnecessary pain as possible."

"I doubt I'll attend, Ms. Blanchard."

I rise and waltz to the door, nudging the balled-up panties toward her with the toe of my Mary Jane as I pass. She picks it up, her face beet-red with embarrassment. I open the door and motion to the sunny day outside. "Yeah, Ms. Waghorn. I think that would be *wise*."

10

The drive to the Computer Depot was a quiet one. Jacoby held the handle above his window with white knuckles like he'd just been kidnapped and forced to sit passenger in a NASCAR race. He didn't say a word when I clipped the curb full of newly-mulched palms. He just stared straight forward out the windshield like he was catatonic.

Admittedly, my style of drivin' takes some gettin' used to, but I still think he's bein' a touch of a drama queen about it. Now that we're inside, browsing the aisles for a new laptop, he seems to have relaxed a bit.

"What about this one?" I ask, pointin' to one of the laptop displays. "Nice and light."

He reads through the spec sheet and scrunches his black eyebrows. "What's it mostly gonna be used for?"

"Emails and video mostly."

"Yeah, that one should work, then." He shrugs like there are better options. He wanders down an aisle a bit and points to one. "This has a better processor. Might not lag so much with the videos. That one you just looked at is kinda trash."

"Alright, I trust ya. Get someone who works here to unlock the cabinet and grab one, would ya? I gotta pick up a few other supplies." I point toward the back of the store and saunter off as he hails someone in a uniform down.

Minutes later, we're standin' in a long line for the only open cashier. Jacoby's holding the box with the reverence of a newborn, and I'm draggin' a corkboard in one arm and holdin' pins, index cards, and markers in the other.

I nudge him with my shoulder. "You doin' okay?"

His smile fades, quickly replaced by a frown. He stares forward at the bald spot of the man in front of him. "Yeah. I'm hangin' in there. Still in shock, I think. It's hard to wrap my head around it all. Trying to be strong for the family."

"Yeah. I know."

"Part of me can't believe he's gone, you know? But, then again, he wasn't a very good person. He's made a lot of enemies over the years."

"You ain't kiddin', kid. Between you, me, and the fence post, last night I told Cosmo I wanted to wring your Daddy's neck myself. Couple hours after you went back to the Lagniappe, Carl had an angry visitor tryin' to bang down my door, hollerin' a bunch of nonsense on my lawn. He punched your daddy square in the face."

"Doesn't really surprise me at this point. It's what Dad does... or... *did*. And Jolene, she's a really nice person. Everyone knew she could do better. That's why this morning, I wanted to be strong. I was doin' that for *her*. She didn't need *two* kids crying on her."

"You're right. She didn't." I purse my lips. This whole situation is bummin' me right out.

"I'm not even gonna be her kid at all now." That sentiment looks like it's hurtin' him deeply. "I was... really looking forward to finally being part of a family."

"Well, son, you already *have* a family," I say as we both shift up a few feet closer to the register.

"Aww, thanks, Gran-Gran."

"No!" I pull back and scrunch my brows. "I meant your mom and stepdaddy."

His face sours. "Pfft. Are you kidding me? Frederick pays me no attention, either. And my mom, well, to her, I was always just a *pawn* to try to win *Dad* back."

I wince. "Ewww. She wanted your dad *back*?"

"Oh *yeah*. She never for a minute stopped pining over him. Really irritated Frederick when they were dating because she still wouldn't take off the ring Dad gave her. Was kinda disrespectful to Freddy, actually."

Hmm. This information piques my interest...

If Jacoby's mother, Lisa, was still obsessed with Carl all these years later, it might've given her or Freddy motive to kill Carl. Freddy might've wanted him out of the picture once and for all. Or Lisa might've found out about Annie

Waghorn or Jolene and had one of those *if-I-can't-have-you, no-woman-can* freakouts.

Jacoby steps forward another three feet, and I drag my board to follow. I'm always blown away by how crazy tall this kid is. I don't even think I come up to his shoulders. Heck, come to think of it, I barely come up to *any* man's shoulders these days.

"Freddy never liked Dad," Jacoby volunteers casually. "Anytime Dad popped up in Mom's life, it would throw Freddy in a sorta tail-spin. Guy's got a real temper, too."

"Do you think… he could have done… *you know*?" I don't know how to phrase it so that it isn't a blatant reminder of what Jacoby's just lost. I'm certain that when it all hits him in a few hours, or even a day or two, he's gonna be inconsolable.

"Dunno." Jacoby shrugs.

Just then, his cell buzzes. He answers on the first ring. The line moves, and we set everything down at the register.

The young clerk rings up all my things as I eavesdrop on Jacoby's half of the conversation, which sounds a little something like this:

"Yes, this is Jacoby Easterly."

"Mmm-hmmm."

"Yes, sir, absolutely. Anything to help."

"Sure thing, my Gran-Gran is about to take me for a bite to eat, but we could swing through a drive-through and come right over."

"Oh, yes, she's right here. Would you like to speak to her?"

"Oh... okay. Yes, sir, we will see you shortly."

After he hangs up, he flashes a tense smile as the clerk gives me my receipt. I stuff it in my alligator-skin purse and gather my purchases.

"Bad news," Jacoby says as he stuffs the phone back in his pocket. "That was Amos. He wants us both to come into the station and give an official statement on the record. You know... for Dad."

I nod as we scuttle toward the Buick, pretendin' to be sad. In truth, this'll get me out of an hour of awkward conversation with my would-be grandson over dinner. Secretly, I'm elated by this news.

"Oh shoot. I was looking forward to spending some time with you," I lie. "Whaddaya say we just grab some Cane's and a daiquiri at the drive-thru and head over? I have a feeling I'm gonna wanna have a little *booze* in me for this. Amos Landry has a way of fryin' my nerves just by existin'."

Jacoby nods and helps me put my things in the trunk. "Hey, Gran-Gran, can I ask you a question?"

I swallow my hatred for the idiotic nickname and nod.

"You think I could drive us? It's just... you're a little scary behind the wheel."

"Kid, didn't anyone teach you to show respect for your elders?"

"I do respect you… it's just… we blew through two stop signs and turned left on a red on the way here."

I glare at him.

"We went the wrong way down a one-way, Gran-Gran."

"Son, when you've been drivin' in Killjoy as long as I have, you develop a sorta sixth sense on which laws are serious and which ones are a li'l loosey-goosey."

He nods and swallows hard. I realize this is terrible advice for a nineteen-year-old out-of-towner, and I hand him the Buick key.

"Tell you what, kid. You agree to never call me Gran-Gran again, and I'll let you drive the tank this one time."

Jacoby's smile slowly returns. "You got it, Uma."

"*That's* more like it, kid."

11

Two chicken finger combos and one lime daiquiri later, Jacoby and I stumble into the dinky Killjoy Sheriff Station. Clara Torelli greets us at the front desk. She puts down her copy of the latest *Enquirer* and smiles, speakin' with a voice that sounds like she's two packs of Pall Malls away from havin' to greet me through a stoma. Even though she's only in her forties, her skin is leathery enough to allow her to get in on all those senior discounts at the *Ihop* without bein' carded.

"Well, well, well. Look what the cat dragged in. If it ain't Uma Blanchard herself." Clara smiles, eyes crinkling like wrapping paper in the outer corners. She bares her tobacco-stained teeth in a way that reminds me of Cocodrie, back when he still had all of them and could still see enough to get excited about things.

"Clara Torelli. I ain't seen you in a dog's age. How ya doin', hun?" I say, shuffling my veiny legs around her desk to give her a friendly half-hug.

She looks at my outfit, a Hawaiian shirt, short sleeve button-down with hibiscus flowers printed all over it, and a pair of elastic-waisted hot pink shorts. I know this get-up's far too jovial for such a reverent occasion, but when I dressed at the hotel, everything else in my suitcase seemed even *more* inappropriate. I couldn't rightly wear a floor-length evenin' gown or a one-piece swimsuit to the Computer Depot, now could I?

Clara looks me up and down. "Well, ain't you somethin' else."

"Oh. My outfit? Yeah, it's a long story, Clara. All I have is what I planned to take on the cruise Saturday after the weddin'."

"Who's getting' hitched? You finally get your flirty little hooks into that stunt man 'cross the street? What's his name again? Gemini?"

"*Cosmo*. And no. I'm a little old to be gettin' married, don't you think?"

She smiles. "Oh, no, Uma. I'm a firm believer that it's never too late for love."

Spoken like a forty-something-year-old spinster-in-training. I have it on good authority that she's been amassin' a herd of stray cats out there on her little redneck bend of the Mississippi.

"It's good to see you," she says, voice growling like tires on those bumpy things on the roadside that wake you up when you fall asleep at the wheel.

Not… that I fall asleep at the wheel… *much*.

"Amos wanted you both to come in and give an official statement. Hold on. Lemme buzz him." She presses a tanned finger against a few buttons on her corded desk phone and speaks lowly, "Mr. Landry, Uma Blanchard is here with…"

Her hazel eyes study Jacoby. He rises from the plastic seat in the shabby little excuse for a lobby and addresses her.

"Jacoby Easterly, ma'am."

"He's Carl's son," I say. Then, I mutter behind the back of my hand. "*One* of 'em, anyway."

She quirks a brow at the second part of that comment and speaks into the receiver. "Jacoby. Mr. Easterly's son."

She listens and nods and then hangs up. "Mr. Easterly, Amos would like to see you first, if that's alright."

"Yes, ma'am." He rises, smooths his T-shirt, and approaches her desk. She points a dangerously long nail toward a door with the words *Deputy Amos Landry* on it. Jacoby disappears inside.

I lean down toward Clara and speak with a hushed voice. "Quick, Clara. What can you tell me about the case?"

"Oh, Uma. I… can't."

"You *used* to!" I grin.

"Yeah, but Uma, back in those days, you weren't a," she looks around and then whispers, *"person of interest."*

"Person 'a interest?" I say at full volume. "I was fast asleep when that poor fool croaked!"

"Shhh! You tryin' to get me busted?" She looks around, debatin' whether she should say more. "Well... couple people have been sayin' you made jokes about wantin' to wring Carl's neck."

I press my fists to my hips, "Clara, if *that* makes someone a person 'a interest, I'd reckon about half the people Carl's ever met is on that list right there *with* me."

"Someone said you made a joke about *voodoo*, about pokin' his doll right in the *head* with a needle."

"First off, darlin', it was just a joke. I don't even know voodoo. My auntie made me swear never to play around with that stuff. She also made me promise never to go huntin' no *rougaroux* either, and I sure didn't. That furry thing can stay buried in the bayou, and that'd be just fine with me."

"Did you say it? The thing about the voodoo and the neck-wringin'?"

"Of *course* I said it! The man is... *was*... infuriatin'! Doesn't mean I was actually gon' do it!"

"I'm sorry, Uma. I really shouldn't say any more."

Heck, she shouldn't have said *that* much. I decide to press her anyway. "What about the autopsy? That report come back yet?"

Clara throws her head back in a gravelly laugh, one that sounds like she should consult with a doctor... and *soon*.

"Uma, Wells is gonna need time for all that. The poor fella was just hauled off to the morgue a few hours ago. Wells probably won't have that report done until Friday. And that's if he doesn't tie one on on Thursday night down at *The Flytrap*."

"What do we know about Clifford Owens so far? Does he have an alibi? He sure was all fired up last night when he came and knocked Carl out on my porch."

"Moses went and interviewed him just after lunch at the refinery. I don't know what Cliff told him." She throws her hands up in the air. "Why am I tellin' you all this, Uma? You always used to do this. It's like you inject me with some kinda truth serum every time you're here!"

I don't inject the girl with nothin'. I just know she's lonely, and nobody around this station spends any time talking to her. The poor girl would blab classified details to a *crossing guard* if he'd just ask one question about the weather.

When Harry was on the force, I used to think her blabbin' was a bad thing. Like havin' a slow leak in your front tire with the way she just trickles information out. But, after a little while, I realized I could use it to my advantage and get the skinny on some of the cases I was trying to help Harry put to bed. The sooner the cases were solved, the more I got to see him around the house. And with a bundle 'a children always runnin' around, I needed the man's presence to keep me sane. Glad to see nothing's changed with Clara in all these years.

"How about this... as a gesture of goodwill and a chance to show you that this ain't just a one-sided secret partnership we got here, I'm gonna give you a brand *new* name."

"I've already got a name. Got a nickname, too. Brother calls me *Chicken-scratch* on account of my poor penmanship."

Clara ain't the brightest bulb in the box. But unlike her dim co-worker Amos, if you see her out and about, she can be a real hoot to hang out with.

"Clara, that ain't what I meant. I'm gon' give you the name of someone *else*. For the *case*. And you're gonna pass it along for Moses to look into."

"*Ohhhh*."

"The name is Annie Waghorn. Long, gray hair, mid-to-late-fifties. Probably two-forty. Little husky."

She starts frantically scribbling the name and description down on a pink notepad, and I can see now why she got the nickname Chicken-scratch. She's got handwritin' worse than any doctor I ever seen. The words don't even look English. Looks like ancient hieroglyphs.

"This Annie Waghorn was," I eye the closed door to make sure it's still shut tight. I don't want Jacoby to hear me speakin' ill of his dead daddy. "She was havin' an affair with Carl."

Clara gasps and shakes the back of her pen at me. I can see it is one of those tip pens where the hunky man in a suit strips down to just silver underwear when it's held upside down.

"You know, I'll bet *that's* who he was cheatin' on *Danielle* with when she divorced him."

"Excuse me?" That name is one I don't think I've heard before. "Who's Danielle?"

"His wife. Well, ex-wife. One of 'em, anyway. The last one. Danielle…" She shuffles through some pages in the tan file on her desk, "I think her last name is Easterly still. Said she hasn't had time to revert back to her maiden name since the divorce."

"I don't remember Jolene tellin' me anything about a woman named Danielle. What's the maiden name?"

She refers to her papers again. "Umm… Martin."

I gasp. "Danielle Martin? The girl whose mama ran off with that contestant from the cookin' show a while back?"

"Yup. The very one. She was married to Carl for a *long* time. Probably about a decade or so, if I remember right."

I feel dazed. I have no *clue* how Carl kept track of all his foolin' around. "No kiddin'! Wow, small world. Why'd they split?"

"Cheatin'. Danielle said he was seein' some girl on the side. I imagine maybe it was this Annie lady."

"When was this?"

"They divorced about, what, eight, nine months ago?"

My stomach flips like I'm on a nauseatin' carnival ride. The math just ain't addin' up. Jolene brought Carl home to introduce him just about a year ago. They'd already been dating for a little while, she said. Heck, they probably didn't even wait for the ink to dry on the divorce papers before they got engaged.

Maybe *Jolene* was the other woman that made him end things with his wife! Oh, dear Lord, I hope that's not the case! I raised Jolene better'n that. At least, I *thought* I did!

"Oh, *cher*, I might have to sit down." I wobble over to the waiting area and plop into a chair.

"You okay, Uma?"

"Yeah, I'll be fine. This all is just so much worse than Jolene made it out to be when she introduced him to the family."

"Yeah, Danielle said Carl was a sneaky one. Said he was pretty much leading one of them-there double lives. Had a second phone and everything."

I shake my head, which feels heavy with the weight of all this dead man's nonsense. "Yeah, Annie said that, too. Said he had a black one and then one with a Hindu-lookin' design."

Clara scribbles some more notes.

"Did they recover one or two phones at the scene?"

"Uma, you know I can't tell you that."

I pout at her. It's all it takes for her to cave like a weak dam.

"Just one. A black one, I think."

I wonder where his second one could be. Then, suddenly, I remember the scream of the woman in the bath a few hours earlier, the look of terror on her face when she saw *me* instead of Carl. I laugh to myself at the image of it all.

"Care to share what's so funny with the *rest* of the class, Ms. Blanchard?"

"Well, it's just… when I checked into Carl's allegedly *spare* hotel room today, Annie was there, soakin' in the tub, naked as a jay-bird."

"Well, *that* had to be awkward."

"That word doesn't even begin to cover it. She was scared outta her mind. She claimed she didn't know Carl was even *dead*. She started cryin' and everything."

"Yeah, but who knows. Sometimes, they're just crocodile tears. If she and Carl were seein' each other a while, I reckon that kinda jealousy is as much a motive for murder as any. I'll have Cheramie check her out, see if she had an alibi."

"She claims she was at work," I volunteer. "Said she's a nurse and was working a late shift. Might be worth checking out if there are any other men in her life who might wanna do Carl in on her behalf."

"Well, if she's a nurse, that'll be easy to corroborate an alibi for where she was around four a.m." She looks down at her papers and then up at me. "They got cameras all 'round that hospital. They'd be sure to catch her comin' and goin'."

"Four o'clock? Was that the approximate time 'a death accordin' to Wells?"

"Whoops." She nods sheepishly. "But you didn't hear that from me."

"That gives me a time frame to narrow things down to, at least." I lean forward. "Jacoby let me in on a little secret, too. Seems his mama still kinda pines over Carl. Seems his stepdaddy ain't too pleased about it either. It might be worth lookin' into. Names are Lisa and Frederick."

"Yeah, the Slaters. I think their name already came up in conversation when Moses started pokin' around."

"I always thought it was strange that Jacoby has Carl's last name, and yet, Carl's barely been around in his life. Seein' them together, Jacoby might as well have been a ghost."

"Hmmm," Clara said like she was thinking about it. And then she didn't say anything after.

A door next to Landry's opens, and Moses steps out into view, hidin' half of his rotund body inside the room. "Clara, you being good out here?"

Clara nods like a child, straightening in her chair.

"You doin' like I asked and keeping your lips zipped about the case?"

She nods, a blatant lie.

"Because I hear you out here talkin' a whole lot." His voice is like a father who finds his child's answer dubious.

"Yes, sir. Uma and I were just talkin' about all the fun stuff she had planned on her cruise."

"Yeah," I chime in bitterly, "you know, the one I gotta call and cancel later 'cause you wanna hold me hostage here by keeping me on standby just in case."

Moses sighs. "Uma, are you here for an official statement?"

I nod. "Landry sent for Jacoby and I."

He waves me into his office and rubs his tired brown eyes. "Come on in. I just finished some paperwork. I'll take it down myself."

12

Back at the hotel, I sit at the desk in my bedbug-riddled room and toe my slippers as I set my computer up. The loadin' screen is taking forever, so I carefully wake Cocodrie and latch the leash onto his harness, one that makes him look much more playful and approachable than he is. The handle on the spine is helpful for yanking him off things when he's hungry for flesh. He looks around as if he can't see me right in front of him. I speak clearly so that he is not surprised when I touch him.

"Cocodrie, I am goin' to take you for a walk now. You haven't piddled since I got back. I'm goin' to lift you off the bed now."

I slowly slide a hand beneath his belly, and he growls. I freeze, my blood turnin' into the consistency of a frozen daiquiri at the sound.

"I am pickin' you up now."

I lift gently, and he snarls. At who? I'm not certain because his fogged eyes are fixated on the hotel door. I lower him to the floor, and he makes the sound of a caged monkey with rabies. I try to yank my hand back before I end up with any injuries.

Another success.

I grab my key card and start out the door, draggin' the dog behind me like a balloon on a string that's all out of helium.

"C'mon, boy. I ain't playin'."

Finally, Cocodrie decides to use his legs and follows me, slidin' through the door just before it closes on his tail.

He looks toward the right, to the block of rooms where Jacoby and Carl's family are stayin', then to the left down a long corridor. He steps to the rail, listening to the splash of children in the pool three stories down. Surely, he can't see them, but I imagine he wants to bite them all just the same for havin' fun.

Cocodrie takes forever to waddle to the elevator, and the sound of the doors closin' sends him into a barkin' fit. As the doors open, I drag him out and tug him toward the grass.

Eddie is there, leaning against the side of the building, the waning light of the evening sky shinin' against his blond hair. Half a cigarette hangs out his mouth, and he speaks without removin' it.

"Hey."

"Hello. Just had to take Cocodrie for a little walk to potty. He needs to stay active."

Eddie nods. "You ever thought about puttin' him down?"

I scoff. "I put him down all the time. Watch." I turn to the Chihuahua, who has his leg lifted like he's peeing, although nothin' is comin' out. "Nobody likes you but me, you dusty old fart."

Eddie laughs, and Cocodrie lowers his leg from a satisfying ghost pee. He sniffs around for another spot to mark with his non-existent stream.

"Your room satisfactory?" Eddie asks.

"It's not the Ritz-Carlton, but it'll do."

"Want one?" He holds up his pack of cigarettes. I haven't smoked since Harold was alive, but today has been a doozy.

"Why not?" I take one from his pack, and he lights the end of it for me. I suck a bit of it back and cough the word "*Yolo*."

Eddie laughs. "Did you just say what I think you said?"

"I'm usin' that right, am I not? Yolo. You only live once?"

"Yep. You're usin' it right. Just never heard someone… like *you*… say it."

"One of my evil grandsons taught it to me. He usually says it right before he shoves his twin off somethin' dangerously high."

"Kids are crazy."

"You're tellin' me. I raised a bunch of 'em."

I take a long drag, and a rush of memories flood back to me from the days when I mindlessly smoked a pack a day, escapin' my job for fifteen minutes here or there to be outside for a bit. It was always a way to reset whatever nonsense was goin' on between my co-workers and me.

"I used to smoke a lot," I say, blowin' out a lungful into the muggy night air.

"I can never seem to quit," Eddie says, angling his foot sideways across his knee and snuffing the butt on his sole. Once it's out, he lowers his foot, and I get a flash of the diamond pattern on the bottom. It reminds me of the bloody footprint in my kitchen this mornin' when I found my future son-in-law as cold as his waffles.

"Those are interestin'." I nod toward his black-and-white checkered shoes.

He looks down at them and laughs. "Yeah. They're Vans, I think. First time ownin' a pair of slip-ons."

"They look just like the ones on that poster for that movie a while back."

"*Fast Times at Ridgemont High?*" He laughs. "I think it's the same ones, now that you mention it."

"They comfortable?"

"No. Not particularly." He chuckles, fidgetin' with the pack of cigarettes like he's debating on firin' up another one.

Eddie smirks. "You aren't a fire-bug, are you, Ms. Blanchard?"

"Well, now, why would you be askin' a thing like that? Seems to me that *you're* the one with the lighter here."

He eyes me suspiciously for a moment.

"What?"

"Nothin'. It's just that I saw smoke last night out back here and…" he looks at his shoes again and waves me away. "Nevermind. Forget it."

"What? Was someone torchin' something in the woods there?"

"Something like that. Ran off before I could get a good look at 'em. What with you bringing up the shoes, I had to ask."

"What's a fire in the woods got to do with a pair of checkered slip-ons?"

"Well, funny enough, I saw the smoke, so I went to go check it out, you know, make sure it didn't spread. I don't want this place to go up like a tinderbox and turn everyone inside into human s'mores."

I wince at the idea of Cocodrie and I in bed, smoke all around us, faces meltin' like marshmallows.

"Someone was burnin' a perfectly good set of tools back there. And so I wave and holler, and the person takes off into the woods. I don't follow 'em too far. There's a gully back there, and it's full 'a gators. It's really dangerous to be messing around back there durin' mating season. They get extra defensive."

I nod and take another drag of the cigarette, watching the tendrils of smoke curl up toward the violet-tinged sky. The night sky around here always has a slightly purple hue to it. Never seen anything like it anywhere else in the world.

"I come back over to the fire to try to put it out. I'm throwing dirt on it, tryin' to stomp it with my boot... and that's when I see this nice-looking pair of Vans right there in the leaf litter. Like this person had just taken their shoes off for God knows what reason and then ended up runnin' off barefoot into the woods."

"Did you call the authorities?"

"Nah," he says, pullin' away from the wall, watching the kids splash in the pool with his hands on his narrow hips. He couldn't weigh more than a buck-thirty soakin' wet. "Probably just kids going through that fire-bug phase. You know."

"You mean future arsonists?" I laugh and toss down my butt on the sidewalk, stomping it out with my house slipper. Cocodrie sniffs it, and I pick it up before the old fool can try to eat it.

"Crazy thing was, the dang things just so happened to be my size!"

"You mind if I see the sole on it real quick?"

He looks at me strangely and then shrugs. He lifts his leg at the knee and holds it up. It looks like the exact same diamond pattern that I saw, although it's hard to know for sure. It wasn't like I was snappin' pictures of it in the heat of the moment. I was a little more focused on Carl's dead body.

"Thank you," I say, making a mental note that now I know the type of shoe sole that makes those patterns. "And thanks for the nail," I say, holdin' up the tan remainder of the first cigarette I've had in nearly ten years.

"Nice talkin' with you. You have a good rest of your night. I'm in the office if you need anything. Just ring the bell." He points back toward the thicket of jungle-like woods behind the Lagniappe Inn and speaks again. "If you see any hooligans lightin' things on fire, you let me know."

"Will do." I salute Eddie.

Cocodrie lets out a warning bark at a wall. Somehow, it has done something to offend him just by existin'. I know how that wall feels…

"I best get this little monster back up there. I got a lot to do."

***

In my hotel room, I scribble some things in permanent marker onto index cards. Cocodrie pretends to watch in my general direction, probably only vaguely aware that anyone else exists in the room with him.

On one card, in big letters, I write the word **SUSPECTS** and pin it to my new corkboard. Then, I start to fill out cards with what I know.

ANNIE WAGHORN
Single. Nurse. One of Carl's mistresses.

Pretended she didn't know Carl was dead. Claims she was working the night shift at the hospital.

I pin her information to the board.

I don't have much on Cliff yet, so beneath his name, I simply write:

CLIFFORD OWENS

Married. Refinery worker. Carl cheating with his wife, Melissa. Baby's paternity is in question. Rage a possible motive. Alibi: allegedly working late shift after the assault.

MELISSA OWENS

Married. Occupation unknown. One of Carl's mistresses. Is Carl the father of her child? Jealousy a possible motive. Alibi: Unknown.

Who else?

LISA SLATER

Married to Frederick. Occupation unknown. Previous relationship with Carl. Pining over him ever since breakup. Alibi: If I can't have you, no one can.

I wrack my brain for other names.

JOLENE BLANCHARD

This one hurts me to write. It isn't right to suspect my own daughter, but who has more of a motive to kill the guy than the bride-to-be who finds out he may have just fathered *another* baby with his co-worker's wife?

JOLENE BLANCHARD
Engaged to deceased. Jealousy a possible motive. Sleeping in the same house at time of murder. Had access to victim.
Alibi: says she was sleeping.

I pin it to the board. In a second column, I make a card with the heading: **CLUES**. Beneath it, I pin cards that say **BLOODY FOOTPRINT - VANS BRAND SHOE.** I also add one that says **MISSING SECOND PHONE. POSSIBLE HINDU DESIGN?**

I also write one that just says: **MURDER WEAPON???**

Then, just for giggles, I write **121906** on another card, just in case I can somehow find his other phone. He might've used the same lock code on both. If I don't write it down, I know I'll forget it when I need it.

I slink down into the chair in front of the laptop, which has finished loading. I use the wi-fi code on the plate screwed into the wall to log onto the internet. I search images of Vans soles and save one. I log into my email and send the picture to Moses Cheramie. I have the emails of everyone at the station. When Harold worked there, I always organized the office holiday parties. No one knows how to host a Mardi Gras party better than Uma Blanchard.

I attach the photo with a message that says:

Moses,

This is the tread of the bloody shoe-print I saw in the kitchen. I think they're Vans. Saw a pair tonight on the kid running the Inn, and the soles looked exactly the same.

Anyway, how goes the investigation? Any leads or alibis I should know about?

-Uma

I send it, and it disappears into the ether with that satisfyin' little *whoosh* sound. Then, I scroll down and smile at an email from Cosmo. Even seeing his name in print makes me grin. His email says:

Hey beautiful,

Here are copies of the footage that you asked for. The angles aren't great, but it certainly caught something.

Cheers,

Cosmo

I shove my notepad and bottles of hot sauce away from the laptop as if they have any bearing on how this device'll function. I click on the first of two attachments, eager to watch the videos to see if there's enough on 'em to nab the person who did this.

There's still time to catch that cruise.

To my dismay, an error screen pops up saying somethin' about how my video player doesn't support the file type. I try the other video. Same message. I lean back in my chair and sigh. Suddenly, I remember I have a boy next door who grew up in the age of this kind of technology. Surely, he could help.

I scuttle out of the room, walking past Cocodrie's blank stare at the paintin' of a *pirogue* on the wall. I rap on Jacoby's door, and I hear the bangin' around of the kid, presumably tryin' to tidy before opening up. It clicks and swings in, and I see the TV playin' some sort of brightly-animated show.

"Aren't you a little *old* for cartoons?"

He sniffles and wipes his reddened eyes with his forearm. Suddenly, I feel horrible. He's in his room trying to mourn, and here I am buggin' the kid for the umpteenth time today.

He clears his throat and composes himself. "It's anime. It's a show for adults."

"You know what, this can wait. I'm sorry to have bothered you."

"No, it's fine. I could use the distraction. What's up?"

Just then, Cocodrie hops down and waddles out onto the concrete, pressing his crusty nose through the iron rails, tryin' his best to peer down at the pool.

I point next door to my room, a little deflated. "You're good with computers, right?"

He chuckles. "Yes."

"Good. Hopefully, I'll only need to borrow you for a second."

He grabs a key card off the dresser and follows me next door. Right away, I start talking.

"I'm trying to get these-here videos to play. They were the whole reason I bought the laptop, and now they won't seem to open."

Cocodrie wafts in, climbs inside my open suitcase, and roughs up the contents in an effort to make himself a lumpy bed on my evenin' gowns and beachwear.

"Oh, Coco, no," Jacoby says, pointing for the dog to get out. "Your mommy's gonna have dog hair all over her clothes!"

"I wouldn't bother. He's set up shop in there." I roll my eyes. "If you try to get him out now, you're gonna end up with one less finger or a bleeding wound on your ankle."

"That dog gets away with murder." Jacoby shakes his head and looks around.

"Yeah," I laugh and point to the cork rectangle propped atop my mini fridge. "Maybe I should put him on the board as a suspect. He was there last night, too."

Jacoby's eyes settle on my scribbled note cards. "Wow. Look at you. *Matlock* over here. All you need is some red yarn and a big Louisiana map, and you'd have the whole *Mindhunter* set up."

I laugh and take a seat at my computer, but Jacoby drifts over to the board instead, studying the intel on the cards intently.

Finally, he says with disbelief, "You really think my *mother* coulda done this?"

"You said she was pinin' over him all this time. Nothin' like the stress of a wedding to make a jealous woman go bonkers."

"Yeah, but Mom wanted Dad back. She waited *this* long. She'd have waited another ten years until he divorced Jolene." Then his eyes grow huge and apologetic. "Sorry, that was rude. I shouldn't have said that."

I scoff. "No. I get it. It's true. Seems to be the way he is… *was*. Seemed like the love-'em-and-leave-'em type through and through. I just think maybe she got tired of waitin' around. Or maybe she heard about Melissa, too."

"Mom wouldn't hurt a fly. She ain't the best mother in the world, but she loved Dad more than anything."

"I doubt that. She had you."

He stares at me, dead-serious. "I mean it. She loved Dad more than *anything*. Including me, Uma. Heck, she didn't even give me her last name when I was growing up. She made my last name the same as *Dad's*. Almost like a present to him or something to show how much she wanted a family with him. Even when she married Freddy and he insisted she take his last name, mine didn't change."

"Wow. That's bizarre."

"I got two half-brothers, too. She and my stepdad had two boys of their own. They both got Freddy's last name. Not me, though."

I let that sink in for a moment. Poor kid is like a man without a country, never feelin' like he belonged anywhere.

"I grew up to be the spitting image of Dad except with hair. Seemed like it only made Mom a little nuttier about the whole thing."

"How so?"

"Well, I heard a while back that Freddy caught her writing letters to Dad. He wanted to surprise her one night by doing all the housework and laundry while she was out and found a bunch of correspondence in the bottom of her underwear drawer. It was pretty *risque*, from what I heard. They were saying they wanted to run off together, leave us all behind and start anew. Maybe start a new life somewhere in the Rockies or something where no one knew who they were." He smirks, but his expression is pained. "She told Dad in the letters that Freddy could keep my brothers, but there was no mention of me anywhere."

"Maybe they were gonna scoop you up and take you, too."

"I was holding out hope that was the case, but Freddy sat me down and said that in the letters, it seemed like they forgot they had a son together. Made me feel kinda... invisible."

He grabs my Sharpie and an index card and makes an addition to my list of suspects.

FREDERICK "FREDDY" SLATER
Married. 41. Violent temper. Hated Carl. Jealous over emotional affair.
Alibi: Unknown.

"There." He tacks it to the board. Then, his head ticks to the side curiously.

"What?"

"Jolene's on here?"

I nod solemnly. "Just because she's kin don't mean she didn't have *motive*. I love my daughter, but she's human like anyone else. If she did this, it still needs to come to light. You can't just run around murderin' men you don't like. You dump 'em like a *lady*."

"Do you really think it's her?"

I shake my head. "Heck no, I don't. I've known Jolene her entire life. She's what we call a *bleedin' heart*. Always givin' money to the vagrants in the French Quarter dressing their dogs up or takin' in strays, *your daddy included*," I joke and then frown at how tasteless that was to say in front of Jacoby. Curse my big yap. I need to stop speakin' ill of the dead. The sole of my slipper ain't tasting too good every time I put my foot in my mouth.

"Until I get more evidence one way or another, Jolene stays on the board."

Jacoby taps the card that says *Second cell phone - Hindu design?*

"I've seen this." He shakes his head in disgust.

"What? You did? When?" I perk up.

"Couple days ago. He was checking my Grandpa into the hotel, and Dad's pocket buzzed. He said he had to take the call. I didn't think anything of it for a few minutes. Dad had me help Grandpa upstairs with his bags. I came back down, and he was talking real hush-hush into it to some woman. He hung up real quick when he saw me, and that's when I caught a glimpse of the back of it and realized it wasn't his normal phone." Jacoby flicks the index card with his middle knuckle hard. "When I asked about it, he lied. Said it was his work phone. Said they made him start carrying that around when he was on-call."

"How did you know he was lying?"

"Well, for one, I know my Dad's job doesn't require him to be on-call."

"How do you know that?"

"Because, unlike him, I listen." He shakes his head. "And why would your job make you carry around a less professional-looking phone than your personal one?"

"You're brighter'n people like your Daddy give you credit for."

"Thanks." He smiles. "It's *Shiva*, by the way."

"Hmmmm?"

He taps the note card. "The Hindu thing on the phone case. In the Hindu Trinity, Shiva is known as the *God of Destruction*." He chuckles. "Seems pretty fitting for Dad. Even in death, it seems like he's content to destroy everything." He laughs a little. "It's a little funny, too. Shiva is considered a master of fertility."

I chuckle. "He really nailed that one. The man seemed to be about as fertile as the Tennessee Valley."

"Some people said Shiva was a polygamist, which might've been the appeal to Dad. But a lot of people say that his wives were all names for the same person." He shrugs. "That's kinda funny, too, seein' as though he named me after someone in the Bible with four wives."

"At least he had the decency to add a 'Y' on the end, I guess. Hey, how the heck do you know all this stuff, anyway?"

He rubs the index card with the phone's login code softly, eyes lingerin' on it for an awfully long time.

"This first semester up at LSU, I took an Asian Studies course."

"You don't say."

"Yep. Also took Calc, Anatomy, Computer Studies, American Poetry, and Spanish I. It was a pretty interesting semester."

"Fascinatin'."

He walks over to the tiny table and eyes the hot sauce. "You should come up there sometime. Audit a class with me. I could introduce you to all the cool kids."

I laugh hard. "Yeah, me back in college at almost seventy years old. That'd be *real* cute." I clear my throat. "So about this video file…"

"Yep. Let me take a look." He squeezes in next to me, shoving my chair toward the wall a little and takin' control of the laptop.

"You probably just need a different file player. What exactly are you trying to play?"

"Cosmo sent me a copy of his security camera footage from last night before he handed everything over to the sheriff today. I wanted to scrub through the footage and see if I could pick up any clues."

Jacoby tries a few things, clicks around for a minute, and gets the same error message I got. He frowns. "Strange. Let me try downloading a different player."

I nod. The sounds of Cocodrie's snoring fills the room. He almost sounds like Harold when he sleeps. I yawn hard and look at my smartwatch, the events of the day catching up with me with a sudden attack of drowsiness.

I listen to the *click-clack* of keys and the disappointing *bleeps* and *bloops* the computer makes every time Jacoby tries to play the file.

"Hmm. I'm having a tough time with this."

"Tell you what, kid. I'm gon' take a shower and try to wash this doggone day off my skin so I can get to bed soon."

"Okay," he says, eyes never straying from the screen. He lifts the laptop in his hands and holds the cord up for me to limbo under as I shuffle out of my corner.

I crank the faucet handle and shut the bathroom door, staring at my tired face before the fog obscures me behind a sheen of opaque gray.

***

After a long, rejuvenating shower, I towel off, don my citrus robe pajamas again, and amble out of the bathroom like a football player in slow motion, jogging onto the field through a tunnel of steam. I am relieved to see that Jacoby is gone, and so is the laptop. In its place is an index card that says in marker:

STILL TROUBLESHOOTING. TOOK IT BACK TO THE ROOM TO PROBLEM-SOLVE. CATCH YOU IN THE MORNING, ~~GAM-GAM,~~ UMA. NIGHT!

I'm relieved that I don't have to entertain him or go through any footage tonight with a fine-toothed comb. Maybe a good night's sleep is just the ticket.

I click on the Channel 8 news, watching the footage on screen like a hawk as they show my overgrown yard, Amos Landry trampling my prolific Black-Eyed Susans without a second thought. I learn nothing new from the reporter.

The next story starts. Somethin' about egg prices and rice having unsafe amounts 'a arsenic. I couldn't care less about any of it. I click the TV off and sit in silence.

Well, maybe not *total* silence. After all, Cocodrie's snores sound like the tiny buzz of a chainsaw.

I click all the lights off around the room except one. From the bed, I take a look at my list of suspects again, thinking about who I want to contact tomorrow morning after I check in on Jolene.

I snuggle into bed and think about how I could annihilate a pint of praline ice cream right now. I glance over to the snacks on the table and notice that I'm now down to only one bottle 'a hot sauce. The second one's gone. Jacoby probably needed it to make some leftovers in his room more palatable. Or maybe it he was anticipatin' needin' it for the breakfast they serve here. God only knows how bland it all is at this joint. Heck, it doesn't matter. It's a small price to pay for havin' the kid get my videos to play.

"Night, Cocodrie," I coo, leanin' over the bed to the deceptive sight of my Chihuahua lookin' like an angel, a little bean curled inside a strapless evenin' gown I planned to wear to the formal Captain's Dinner on the Aspire.

13

I awaken to the sounds of heavy room doors slamming in slow succession. Engines rev as lucky people check out of the hotel and go on with their lives. I, however, am still stuck here. Once my dentures are in and my white hair is tamed, I put a leash on Cocodrie and tug the grumpy dog outside for his mornin' wee. Once we make it the half-a-million steps down to the ground level, we head to a grassy spot near the parking lot. Cocodrie sniffs every conceivable leaf he can reach while I watch a grown man cry against a woman's shoulders. They are both around my age, dressed in black. Cocodrie barks at them… *always in favor of adding insult to injury, that one.*

The sound draws the attention of the weeping gentleman. He looks over at me and, then, at the dog, who is now suddenly dropping a deuce *right* by my doggone slipper. My hands fumble the leash in search of my attached dispenser of dookie bags. It only takes a moment to remember that this leash ain't *mine*. It's the loaner from Cosmo, and I'm now wholly unprepared for what to do with the mess. I can't rightly just leave it there, 'specially with people starin' right at me.

I look around for a piece of trash to pick it up with so that I don't look like a steaming pile of the *same* in front of this blubberin' man and his woman. They see my panicked scramble, and the man waltzes over with a newspaper, wipin' his eyes on his forearm.

"Need something to clean that up?" He sniffles, handing it to me as he tries to compose himself.

"Yes, please." I feel like the weight of the world has been lifted off me as he hands it over, knowing that I don't have to leave it for some person to step on or move it to the trash with my bare hands. I shudder at the *thought*! "*Cher*, you're a lifesaver."

He scoffs. "Well, at least I could save *someone's* life. Couldn't save my son's."

Killjoy is far too small for this kinda comment to be a coincidence.

"You... wouldn't happen to be related to Carl Easterly, would you?"

The man looks at me strangely. "What, do I have some sort of sign on my head? How would you know that?"

I pick up the steamin' poo with the comics, careful to avoid Cocodrie, who is sneerin' evilly at me for invadin' his personal space. I walk it a few feet toward the round-top trash receptacle and set the rest of the newsprint on top, just in case Cocodrie wants to go for round two. He did eat some of my leftovers last night…

"You just… seem like you're in mournin', and I remember Jacoby said Carl's parents were in the rooms at the end of the walkway." I point up to the rooms near mine on the third floor.

"John Easterly. That's my wife, Selma, over there." He points to his wife. Then, he sticks out a broad hand to shake mine. He's buff. Looks like he used to play quarterback for LSU or Tulane or somethin', but his accent suggests he ain't from around here. Somewhere up north, probably. His white hair shimmers against the cloudy sky, one that might open up and let loose this afternoon if the dull pain boltin' through my knees is any indication. Some days, these old bones can call an incoming storm with more precision than that handsome weatherman, Trunky Cordon, on Channel 8.

I go to shake John Easterly's hand and reel back, transferring the leash into the one that just held excrement and awkwardly shakin' with the other so as to be more polite. "Uma Blanchard. Carl was engaged to my daughter, Jolene. I'm very sorry for your loss."

"So… you were there?" He gets choked up again.

"Yes, Sir, I was sound asleep when it happened, in one of those deep *Ambien* comas, unfortunately. Well, not unfortunately… 'cause that's actually what the medication's *for,* you see."

He shakes his head, eyes teary again. "I guess we have to stay until Saturday either way. But, instead of going to a wedding," his voice cracks, "we'll be attending a funeral."

He sobs again, and I reach out and squeeze his forearm -- which is like granite rock. *How much does this guy work out?* My goodness, if he didn't already have a wife...

"Sir, I assure you, my sister Cindy is already hard at work on giving Carl a *beautiful* service. She's had a number of husbands and friends die over the years. She's a pro at this sorta stuff. Carl'll get nothing but the best. Thing'll probably end up costin' just as much as the wedding if I know Cindy."

He sniffs hard and wet and wipes his eyes again. "We really appreciate that. Let us know if we can help in any way." He looks back at his wife, then to me. "You happen to know where the sheriff's office is around here? He called. Wanted us to come in and talk on the record."

"Of course. He ain't far. Just go straight down Louis Armstrong 'bout five miles and take a left onto King Cake Road. You'll see it right there. It's an ugly brown buildin'. Can't miss it."

"Thanks, Ms. Blanchard."

"Absolutely." I nod. "And don't you worry, I've been working in an *unofficial capacity* to catch whoever did this to your boy. Not for any selfish reasons of my own," I lie. "Just because I believe in justice and I got a lot more free time on my hands because'a this."

"Well, that is awfully kind of you."

"I wanna make sure you, Jacoby, and all of Carl's kids on the way get some closure in all of this."

"Wait, what?" He is confused. "What do you mean all of Carl's kids on the way?"

Oh, shoot. I've put my foot in my mouth this time! *Quick, Uma. Backtrack. Backtrack!*

"Uh…" I start backing away. "Oh shoot, I think I left my tub runnin'."

I start walking backward quickly and bump into the trash can, scaring the bejeezus outta me.

"Wait, Ms. Blanchard…"

I am in a half-sprint now. "Can't believe I left it on. My room's gonna get soaked. Oh, man, I'm gettin' so forgetful in my old age!" I lie again. As I make it to the stairs, I realize I am draggin' Cocodrie like a yo-yo with a tangled cord through the grass behind me. I stop and let him right himself. He looks completely unfazed, oblivious as to how he just teleported to his new, blurry surroundings.

"Nice to meet you, Mr. Easterly!" I yell across the small patch of grass. The Chihuahua and I make our agonizingly slow ascent to the third floor. I should have taken the elevator. Mr. Easterly watches us the entire way up with a look of confusion all over his face.

Once upstairs, I swipe my card and duck into my room.

Once a couple minutes pass, I peek back outside. Their car is gone, thank God. I prop my door open with the flip latch and stand in front of Jacoby's room. He's gotta be awake by now. I *knock three times* and hum the Tony Orlando song in my head. I think about how, if I wrapped this investigation up quickly, I could still make it to the Aspire in time to slay at karaoke with a classic like that. I could have the whole crowd eatin' outta my wrinkled hands.

I hear a lotta ruckus and a sleepy, "One minute!" Then, I hear some thumps and a stream of obscenities uttered in a growl. Finally, Jacoby opens the door, and I gasp at his appearance. His eyes are bloodshot, ringed red, tears streamin' down both cheeks. He covers his mouth, cryin' so hard that he can barely keep his eyes open.

"Good Lord, Jacoby. I am *so* sorry to bother you!"

His voice is shaky. He tries to sniffle but winces and starts to double over in another bout of tears. "What is it, Uma?"

The kid is clearly in pain. I feel so bad for him. Carl never struck me as the kinda guy worth sheddin' a single tear over, but I guess he was still this kid's father. Heck, even the baby in Jolene's belly might have the same reaction one day thinkin' back on all this. I have never been a pillar of comfort in melancholic times of need, even with my own children. I have always been one to focus more on the *bottom* tier of Maslow's hierarchy 'a needs. Water, food, shelter, clothing. I kept my babies' bellies full. Got 'em educated. Made sure they had all of the basics.

Unfortunately for Daniel, Roxanne, Maggie May, Mandy, and Jolene, when it came to scary dreams or mourning the death of a family pet, I was always a bit useless. Never was very good with that stuff. Emotions and psychological needs were where *Harold* excelled. He was always a source of strength and comfort in the dark times.

"I'm... sorry to have bothered you, Jacoby. I was just checkin' to see if you had any luck gettin' the videos to play on the laptop."

"I tried a bunch of different players. I think the files might be corrupt." As he shakes his head, I get a waft of somethin' pungent, like... cleaning chemicals or...

Vinegar?

Almost as if on cue, a cleaning lady wheels her cart out of room 310 and gives us a polite wave.

She knocks on 309. "Housekeeping."

"Thank you for tryin', kid." I turn back to Jacoby.

"I'll keep troubleshooting. It would give me something to do today. Can't really do much else until after the funeral when I can go back to Baton Rouge."

"No, don't worry yourself over it. I've troubled you enough. I'd like to get it back so I can use it to look up a few other things today."

He studies me for what feels like a long time through those thinly-slit, watery eyes. He grabs a tissue out of his pocket and uses it to dry them. He stuffs it back in his shorts and starts to cry again while nodding. "Yeah, let me get it for you."

He walks over to a table identical to the one in my room, grabs the laptop, and wraps the cord around it. He hands it back to me and stands there in the door, hugging his own chest, silly meaningless tattoos up his arm, the spittin' image of his dad.

"What... are you wearing?" he says with slight disgust.

"Oh, this?" I billow out the bottom of my neon hot-pink Hawaiian shirt with green palm leaves patterned all over it. My shorts are the same bright green as the leaves, and my ghostly-pale legs are on full display beneath the hem, blindin' everyone. Hot pink sandals adorn my feet, my toenails painted a similar color. "Hey, lay off me. I was goin' on a cruise! I'm not buyin' a whole new wardrobe just 'cause I'm stuck here in Killjoy while those stooges at the sheriff's office bungle everything."

He forces a smile, and then it falls. An awkward silence fills the air between us, and frankly, my neck is getting a little tired from staring straight up at the boy. Good *Lord*, he's tall.

I purse my lips. "Well, I got a lot of errands to run today. You got my number. Ring if you need me to bring you anything back. Y'know, food and such."

He nods, tears dribbling down his chubby cheeks again, mouth wrinkling into a half-frown-half-howl, only silent.

"Oh... and... I hate to ask this of you. But, since you're gonna be here all day, do you mind taking that toothy little bear trap covered in fur for a walk after lunch so he can tinkle?"

Jacoby blinks, and another torrent of water rushes from his beet-red eyes. "Sure."

14

SMASH! The sound of my Buick Century careening into Liv and Cindy's black rolling trash bin echoes throughout the neighborhood. I don't even know where the dang thing came from! Musta rolled right in front of me as I was parkin'!

I get out. Liv is there on the porch, arms crossed, watching me.

"You hit the bin again. The city said they won't keep replacing them, Uma. Next one's comin' out of your pocket."

"Yeah, yeah." I scramble to pick up the spilled rubbish and the array of stubby Abita Purple Haze bottles from the now-littered hellstrip in front of her manicured lawn. Then, I right the downed bin onto its wheels. The lid dangles loosely, but it's otherwise still functional. I stuff the trash back in and dust my hands off on my beach shorts.

"There. Good as new."

"Hardly," she says with an eye roll.

"You're judgin' me awful harshly for someone with that much beer in the trash."

"You know I drink beer when I'm stressed," she huffs. "You also know I got a screamin' baby in the house as of late."

Liv's face changes from a disapproving frown into a fake smile. She waves to someone behind me. I look over my shoulder and glare at the cameraman for Channel 8 as he stuffs his face with a fried chicken thigh in front of my wide-mouthed bass mailbox, using the bottom jaw as a holder for his thirty-two-ounce Big Chug. He is waving to her with a glistening hand, mouth full of deep-fried meat.

I yell at the cameraman, "Sir, if you break my fish with 'at drink, I'll kick *your* mother-lovin' bass. Understand?"

"*What*?!" he yells in protest with a shrug. "What's the problem?!"

"I'll complain to Channel 8 so fast it'll make your head spin, boy. I'm retired. I'll mount a full-blown crusade to *ruin* you. I *have* the time."

The man removes the drink with his oily mitts and sets it on the ground, rolling his eyes. "Happy?"

"Son, I'm sixty-eight years old. My body hurts, and every day, I'm one step closer to death. So, no, I don't imagine I am just as a general rule'a thumb."

I turn toward Liv, and her smile has dissipated again. "What on *earth* are you wearin', Uma?"

"Oh, lay off. All I got's cruise clothes."

"Lord almighty, a man just died. I know you ain't sad he's gone, but maybe for your daughter's sake, you show a little respect." She motions down to her black tank top and matching gauze pants, presumably to illustrate I should be dressed in a similar fashion.

"Liv, the only thing in my suitcase that's black is a full-length sequin evenin' gown I was gonna wear to the Captain's Ball. Would *that'a* been more appropriate?" I ask, shuffling along the flower-lined paver path toward the patio.

"Surely, there has to be something in your bag more formal than this. Heck, what do you even *call* this look? You look like you're goin' to a Maui rave."

"I got a one-piece swimsuit and a sarong and a buncha clothes like this. Would you have rather I came over in that?" I climb the steps to the porch, one with a two-person chain swing, slats freshly painted purple, green, and yellow, the colors of Mardi Gras. "Anyway, *Cher*... how's my baby holdin' up?"

"As good as can be expected, I suppose. She's a strong girl."

"Yeah, she is. But is she too strong? That's what I need to find out."

"Whaddaya mean?"

"I mean, is she bein' strong because she's a Blanchard?" I ask, my voice lowering to nearly a whisper. *"Or because she had somethin' to do with his demise?"*

"You think she did ol' Carl in? Over… what? Jealousy?"

"Maybe. Liv, she found out hours before Carl died that he's been puttin' babies in women like they was little *king cakes*!"

Liv looks stunned. "She didn't say anythin' about that."

"Of course not. It's embarrasin'. Did she tell you anything about how originally she was the other woman when they first started datin'?"

"What?!"

"Yeah, I jus' found out yesterday myself. There was some… overlap. Carl and his last wife divorced less than a year ago."

"But Jolene's been datin' him—"

"I *know*. Heck, with how far along she is with dat new baby, I wouldn't be surprised if it was conceived while 'at dead *dum dum* was still married!"

"Oh dear God, I feel lightheaded," Liv says, lowering herself into the seat of the swing.

"He was seeing a woman named Melissa while Jolene was pregnant, apparently. Her hubby came and clocked Carl right in the face the night 'fore he was killed, screamin' about how *his* newborn might be Carl's."

"Lord!"

"Then, there's this floozy named Annie…"

"*Annie*?! Another'n? Oh, Lord, have mercy."

"Who knows how many more there are. Plus, Jacoby's mom, Lisa, was apparently still gaga over him. It's a friggin' mess, *Cher*."

"Well, Uma, you best go inside and see her. She and Cindy are pickin' out headstones. Cindy's ready to spring for the Cadillac of caskets, too, so if you can talk her outta doin' that, I'd appreciate it. She won't listen to me."

"Shoot. Doubt she'll listen to me either."

Liv and I head inside, where Payzlee crashes headfirst into Liv's shriveled shins with a force that dang near knocks her over like a bowlin' pin.

"Payzlee! Careful, baby!" Liv shouts, plucking the diapered child off the ground with a grunt and headin' down the hall.

I shuffle off in the opposite direction where Cindy is, sittin' at the kitchen table, pointin' to a brochure. Jolene is next to her, blue eyes swollen like she lost a vicious bar fight.

"Lord, Jojo, you look terrible."

I can't help my brutal honesty sometimes. Things just fly out of my mouth without a second thought.

…Or, heck, sometimes even a *first* thought.

"*Thanks*, Ma," Jolene growls.

"We can pick this up later, Jo," Cindy coos, strokin' Jolene's shoulder-length blonde hair lovingly.

"If y'all are picking out headstones, you might wanna let Carl's folks have a say in the matter. Met 'em this mornin' while Cocodrie was doin' his business. They're my neighbors over there at the Lagniappe. They're staying through the funeral."

"We're havin' it Saturday. Nice, tasteful service. Lots of peace lilies. Picked him out this gorgeous cream-colored casket for them to put him in once he gets moved over to the mortuary."

I plop down in a vacant chair at the table. "I'll find out exactly when that is today. I'mma pay Wellsy a visit here in a bit and see what I can find out."

Cindy nods, her eyes flitting to Jolene as she bursts into a sob.

"I'll give you two some alone time." Cindy starts out of the room.

"Got any coffee?" I ask, leaning on the rear two legs of the chair, just enough to not teeter backward to the floor.

"Your mind is slippin', Uma. We've done *been* over this. I got *tea*."

I grumble. "Oh yeah, that's right. Antioxidants and gut health and all that nonsense."

Cindy rolls her eyes and leaves. I turn to my daughter and watch for a while until her sobbing subsides.

"I'd ask how you're holdin' up, but that seems like it'd be a real dumb question."

Jolene's eyes meet mine, and they're filled with anger. I'm not sure if it's at me, the comment, or the situation in general.

"Payzlee brought me her iPad this morning," Jolene starts, gritting her molars as she talks, "she started pokin' at it like she couldn't get her cartoons to play. That's when I realized she'd somehow gotten outta the video app and into a *messaging* app."

I nod, listening intently, curious as to where this story is going.

"So I took it from her, and I realized it's linked to some kinda *cloud* where all of our accounts were listed. I saw an account on our family plan I didn't recognize, so I clicked it and started scrollin' through, readin' the messages... It was Carl's! Apparently, he had a second phone on our flippin' family plan this whole time!"

I nod.

She looks at me like I just slapped her. "Wait, you *knew*?!"

I throw my hands up defensively, "I did. I found out yesterday about it. As far as I know, Moses ain't been able to locate it yet." I think about Annie Waghorn, sobbing about it in nothin' but a towel, and I freeze, tryin' to think fast. "Jacoby told me about it. Said it's got a different phone case than the other'n. He told Jacoby it was a work phone for days when he was on-call, but Jacoby said the way Carl was talkin' clearly wasn't work-related."

"Carl's job didn't have him on-call! Oh my God," she starts to bawl, "does *everyone* know more about my relationship than I do?! What the hell?!"

I glance over my shoulder to make sure Payzlee isn't within earshot. She isn't. I lean in toward Jolene. "Jacoby said it's got a Hindu God on it. Shiva."

Jolene looks at me strangely. "He's... got a tattoo of Shiva on his calf, too." More tears fall from her eyes. "I mean, he *had*."

"So... what was in those messages on the cloud thingy?"

She cries harder, so hard I almost can't even understand her next words, "Ma, he was cheatin' on me! With... more than one woman!"

Instead of pretendin' this is some sort of revelation, I lean in closer. "Jolene, I gotta ask you something, but I don't want it to rile you up."

"What?"

"Did you start seein' Carl... while he was still married to a woman named Danielle?"

Jolene slams her forehead against the table so hard that her teacup, full of brown gut water, rattles against the saucer it's on. With her face still against the wood, she says, "I didn't know until later, Ma, I swear! He said he was already divorced. Said they'd been separated for years, that there was no love there." She raises her head to look at me. "And I believed him!"

With one singular angry flourish of her hand, she sends the antique cup and saucer flying, shattering it like a white firework against the kitchen cabinets, splashing gastrointestinal tea and hunks of porcelain on the linoleum floor tiles.

Jolene's burst of anger is executed with such venom that I'm certain she *does* still belong on my suspect board at the hotel. No one can confirm she was *actually* asleep like she said she was 'cause the only person other'n me who coulda vouched for her's *dead*. With her fiancee havin' all these dalliances all 'round Killjoy, she had just as much a reason as anybody to put Carl down for his long dirt nap. Plus, Jolene's a fierce and formidable woman when she wants to be.

If you don't believe me, just ask what's left of that teacup!

Cindy bolts into the room in a panic. "What was that?!"

I flash her a sharp glance. "She broke a cup, Cindy. Send me a bill. I'll buy you a whole new set if you just go away for a minute."

She shouts as she storms off, "Uma Mae Blanchard, you are one rude S.O.B."

"Don't talk about our mama like that," I holler, just to be sassy.

Jolene continues. "Danielle is one of the women he's been writing to! And then there's Melissa, who just had a baby, and now, who knows if it's her husband's or Carl's at this point. It's such a mess!"

"Yeah, and don't forget about *Annie*."

Jolene looks at me like I'm an alien hitchhiking down a Roswell highway. "How'd you know about Annie?! Did you know all this time?"

"No, *Cher*, this was another of yesterday's little surprise discoveries. I found Annie *naked* in my hotel room bathtub yesterday. Apparently, that's what the extra hotel room was for. To make matters worse, he was havin' these little rendezvous five feet from his own son."

"Oh, God, I'm gonna throw up, Ma." She clutches her stomach.

I leap up and scuttle around the broken shards of cup on the floor. At a loss, I grab the only container I can find: a porcelain cookie jar. I remove the lid and hand it to her. "Here. In case you gotta upchuck."

As I set it down in front of her, I see the contents. Pinwheels. One of my *favorite* snacks.

Heck, I didn't lose my real teeth for *no* reason!

I grab two of the chocolate-covered marshmallow treats and sit, tearing into the first one, enjoying the squish of it between my tongue and the roof of my dentures. I moan at the taste and then remember my daughter's distraught, so I straighten my posture and scrunch my brows into a serious expression, shoving the rest of the first pinwheel in my mouth, whole.

"This just... sucks! He was telling us all the same things. Some of the letters to Annie and Melissa where he was talking about wantin' to run off into the sunset with 'em were written on the same day, and it looked like he *copied and pasted* 'em and just changed the names!"

I can't believe how ridiculous this all is. They all fell for his *alleged* charm hook, line, and sinker. They only heard what they wanted to and blocked any sane notion that threatened that theory.

"There was even one person who was writin' him, tryin' to start something up, but Carl seemingly wasn't takin' the bait. Seemed like he was stringin' her along just enough to keep her interested but not enough to juggle her into his little *harem*, at least accordin' to the letters I saw. Who *knows* what he was tellin' her in person, though."

"And who was that?"

"Jacoby's mom. Lisa Slater."

"Oh boy. You know, Jacoby said somethin' to me yesterday about her not bein' over Carl, and it makin' his stepdaddy mad as a mama gator."

"Carl said she was always tryin' to get him back and that she was desperate to rekindle things. So, I always kept my eye on her. I was worried at first, but he made it seem like that kinda desperation was such a turn-off to him."

"Not sure anything was actually a turn-off to *that* boy."

"Ma!" She shakes her head. "They were married a long time ago and had Jacoby a few years before he'n Danielle got together, *allegedly*. Although, I'm findin' out not a word outta that man's mouth ever seemed to be the truth. I'm startin' to wonder if Danielle was even the other woman with Lisa. Maybe Carl's literally never been alone a moment of his entire adult life."

"Well, now he's got the rest of eternity to be alone." I lick the remnants of pinwheel from the corner of my lips.

"Good! It's what that scumbag deserves!"

I study her for a moment. Wondering if my own daughter could be capable of cold-blooded murder. Finally, I say, "Still got that iPad?"

She nods. "Of course."

"Had to ask." I point to the shattered bits of saucer and cup on the floor. "Wasn't sure if this was some sorta trend today. I *do* know how much you love to break things."

"Oh, give it up, Ma! That ol' grandfather clock took up too much space anyhow! I told you I got a rock stuck in my skatewheel. It was an accident. Coulda happened to anyone."

"Yeah, let's glaze over the fact that you were rollerskatin' inside my house and shattered a family heirloom handed down to me from your granddaddy...."

"I was sixteen! Get over it! I bought you a new clock."

"Yeah, a cuckoo clock that scared the living daylights out of me for months. Thanks so much for all the gray hair *that* little gem caused me!" I eye the second pinwheel in front of me, battling my desire to unhinge my jaw like a python and swallow it whole. "I'd like to borrow the iPad, see if I can find any more clues in it, then I could give it to the sheriff in case it could aid their investigation at all."

"Pfft." She stands and stomps toward the living room. She returns with the electronic device, droppin' it in front of me with a clatter right where my second pinwheel was.

(I crammed it in my mouth while she wasn't lookin'.) "Here. Take it. I don't ever wanna see that thing again."

I swallow the sugary lump and move my mouth like Cocodrie after a spoonful of peanut butter, dry and smacking. "These are expensive, *Cher*. I'll just tell Moses to wipe the messages before he gives it back."

Jolene sweeps up the broken porcelain in the kitchen and wipes up the tea with a dishrag. She wrings it out at the sink and stares out the window at the incoming storm clouds. "I think... I'm glad he's dead."

The way she says it is chilling. She pats her protruding belly.

"Whoever killed him saved me from makin' another huge mistake."

"Do me a favor. When your baby comes out," I start out the kitchen doorway, "don't refer to it as a big mistake. 'Least not in earshot, okay? Tends to hurt a kid's feelings when they know they ain't wanted. If you don't believe me, just ask Jacoby."

Her face becomes solemn. "How's he holding up?"

"Eh. Yesterday, he seemed fine, weirdly so. But I knocked on his door today, and the poor kid looked like he'd been sprayed with bear mace."

"I'll call him today to check-in. See if he wants to say a few words at the funeral."

"Did Carl at least leave you or Jacoby any life insurance as a bright side in all this mess?"

She quirks a brow at me and tilts her head. "I don't know. Doubt it. Carl wasn't really a planner. Lazy as hell with any kinda paperwork. Hell, anything that required effort, really. But you never know. I'll look into it."

"You do that." I blow her a kiss from across the kitchen. "Love you, baby."

"Love you, too."

I fish a hundred bucks cash outta my purse and wave it at Cindy as I start out the front door.

"What's that?"

"It's a hundred-dollar bill, you dope."

"I know what it *is*. I meant, what's it *for*?"

"For a new tea set."

"New tea set doesn't cost a hundred dollars, Uma."

"I know. The extra's so's you can get a cheap coffee maker and a can of flippin' Folgers while you're gettin' the tea set. That way, I'll have somethin' to drink when I come over other'n that brown swill you call tea."

"You just walk around with hundred-dollar bills in your purse?"

"Of course."

"You're a little old lady. A stiff wind could best you, girl. You're gonna get robbed flashin' cash like that around!"

"Most of the time, I got Cocodrie to protect me."

She scoffs and takes my cash. "Hell, Uma, if you died, that dog'd eat your face right off your skull before anyone found you."

"I doubt he'll even wait until I'm dead, Cindy. I seen the way he watches over me as I sleep sometimes. He's just bidin' his time 'til he can strike. It's just a game now to see which one of us old fogies outlasts the other'n."

15

"You're soaked, Uma Mae. You look like a nutria," Wells says, eatin' a foam cup of gumbo that's nestled into the crevice of a black body bag, presumably somewhere near the dead person's unmentionables. Fortunately, the corpse inside is *far* too thin to be Carl.

"That your way of flirtin', Wells? Because if so, I got some *notes*." I raise an eyebrow at him. "And just in case no one has told ya, it's disgustin', you eatin' off a corpse like that." I point to his bizarre choice of cup holder.

He smiles broadly and leans back on his stool, charming as ever. "You sure know how to putt the killjoy in… well, Killjoy."

I roll my eyes. "You got a towel or anything? It's rainin' cats and dogs outside."

He points to a small hand towel on a hook by the large metal sink, and I snatch it up, cleaning the reading glasses on the chain around my neck with it before wiping down my face. It stinks of formaldehyde.

"Yeah, we're just now gettin' the tail end of that tropical depression that slammed into Houston, I think." He points down to his gumbo. "You want some? I have some that ain't been anywhere near any bodies that I could heat up for ya. My sister makes it. Her husband's Creole, and it is *legit*."

"I'll pass. Saving myself for *Mike's* later."

"Mmmmmm, po boys. I haven't been to *Mike's* in a minute. That adorable Vietnamese broad still workin' the counter?"

"Tweet? Yup. She practically lives there."

"Got a mind like a steel trap, that one."

"Don't I know it? I ordered food *one time,* and ever since, she recalls my name and order to a 'T.'" I nod to the wall of silver pull-out drawers. "Wells, we go way back."

"Like car seats." His million-dollar grin of bright-white teeth twinkle beneath his curled, white mustache. "Is this about Easterly? Because you know I can't—"

"We *could* play this game where you pretend you can't divulge information to me because I'm a person of interest in the case, then I *could* counter with a spiel about how you used to give me the skinny on all'a Harold's active cases. Then you *could* say somethin' 'bout how that was then and this is now, and then I *could* offer to barter with you. Then we *could* go back and forth on that 'til we come to some mutually beneficial agreement." I shrug. "Or…"

"*Or?*"

"Or we could cut to the chase, and you could tell me what it's gonna take. Then, we could discretely go about our day pretendin' you tried not to say anything."

"You think you can come in here and just cut through all the bull-crap, huh?"

I press my arms onto the edge of the table with the body bag and give him my most flirtatious smile. "Mmmmm-hmmmm. Like a hot knife through butter."

"Where's the fun in that." He winks.

"Wells…"

"Let's say I counter by askin' for a date."

I laugh. "Wellsy, we've been down that road before..."

"Not with *you*. I meant with your sister, *Liv*."

"Oh…"

"She's pretty enough to be my next ex-wife." He chuckles at his own joke and then shakes his head, staring off longingly. "Good golly, I had me a crush on that girl since junior high. To this day, she *still* turns me down every time I ask, like I'm riddled with the plague. I jus' *know* if I could get her on the back of my chopper, she'd fall in love with that thing. And, then, eventually, with me," he swoons.

"You *still* ride that beast of a machine?"

"Every day. Rain or shine."

"Good Lord, Wells, I thought you got hit a while back, and it busted you up real good."

"Sure did. Some out-of-towner in a minivan smacked right into me coming outta Harrah's on Canal Street. Crushed my pelvis. Had to get pins put in my leg. Got a metal *rod*," he bobbles his white eyebrows with a crass grin.

"Dare I ask where?"

"In my *leg*. Don't be a pervert," he jokes.

"And you still got right back on that thing?"

"Well, not that *exact* thing 'cause it's a crushed hunk'a scrap metal now. Rest in peace," he makes a sign of the cross. "No, I got me a nicer one now with the insurance money. I'd like to take Liv out on it one of these days, maybe take her for a cruise 'cross Pontchartrain or to Lafayette for lunch across one'a them long bridges."

I shake my head and think of how lightning-fast Liv is gonna say no when I ask. "Liv, huh? Pfft. You always *did* like the difficult ones." I shrug. "I can try my best, but I'm not her. I can't force her to say 'Yes.'"

"Work your magic with your sister and throw in a couple jars of that homemade strawberry jam you grow in your backyard, and we got a deal." He points at me. "But you gotta really *try* with Liv. You can't just ask her and shrug it off and say you did your best. I'm riskin' my job here."

"I wouldn't wish Liv on my worst enemy, but if that's what tickles your fancy, Wells, I vow to do my best."

He nods and gulps down another heaping spoonful of gumbo.

"So, quit stallin'. I got a lotta stops to make today. Give me the rundown."

He narrows his eyes. "Give me the strawberry jam."

"For someone with a medical degree, you can be awful dim, Wellsy. I don't walk around town with jars of jam *on my person*. It's at my house, which, as you well know, is an off-limits *crime scene* right now! Help me with this, and as soon as I get back in, I'll give you all the doggone jams you want. You'll be drownin' in jam, Wells. You have my word. I got a nice blackberry one you'd love, too."

"Mmm. I do love me some blackberries." He scans me head-to-toe for a moment and then seems satisfied like I somehow just passed his lie detector test. "Alright, fine."

"*Goodie*."

Wells leaps up, always so spry and leprechaun-like in his movements. He grabs a couple of X-rays off his desk, puts one against the lightbox, and hits a switch. The wall lights up. The bones in the back of a skull are caved in.

"I assume this is Carl's noggin we're lookin' at here," I say unflinchingly.

"Yup. Sorry for your loss, by the way."

"Trust me, it wasn't a loss."

"Oof. That's ice-cold, Uma Mae."

I shrug and examine the X-ray.

"Time 'a death was somewhere between four and four-thirty a.m. on Wednesday morning. Carl had two irregularly-shaped lacerations, both within an inch of each other, on the right parietal scalp." He taps the X-ray with the handle of his gumbo spoon and then uses it to circle a spot. "There was a lot of ecchymosis right around here."

"In lay, *Cajun* terms, please."

"*Bruisin'*." He switches the image out for another X-ray, a side view. "In here, there was some tissue-bridging and jagged edging that is consistent with two blows from something like the claw side of a hammer. Actual cause 'a death was blunt force trauma."

He eyes me suspiciously.

"What?"

"You taken inventory of the hammers in your home recently, Ms. Blanchard?"

"Oh, please!" I laugh. "I don't keep hammers 'round my home. When Harold died, I gave every single 'a of them to my son, Daniel. He thought it was a real nice gesture, but I had an ulterior motive."

"What's that?"

"Any time I wanna see him, I just have to break somethin' he can fix or buy somethin' he needs to build for me. Got him to come over for Thanksgiving last year by treatin' myself to one of those television wall-mounts."

"Did you really," he laughs.

"Sure did. I almost never watch TV anymore, either. Just the nightly news because that weatherman, Trunky Cordon, is such a fine specimen."

"I'll take your word on that. All the ladies in Killjoy seem to get twitterpated over that guy." He makes a face. "Personally, I don't trust men who don't have a mustache."

"You wouldn't." I lightly tap his perfectly curled one with my finger, but it's so full of product it doesn't move. "Good Lord, Wells, what do you got in there? Hair spray?"

"It's a proprietary blend. I can't divulge my beauty secrets."

"So," I change the subject and walk around his autopsy table, tinkering with the handle of a plugged-in bone saw. "A hammer, huh? That's interesting."

"Yes, hammer or somethin' similar. The lacerations were curled, so that's what leads me to believe..." He pauses, stoppin' himself from passionately ramblin' on about the convoluted details of his craft. He simplifies his thoughts with the comical bob of his head. "*Yes*. I'm certain it was a hammer."

I use a speculum to point at the body bag on the rolling stretcher where his gumbo waits, steam risin' from the folds of the sunken, black material. "Who's this poor sap?"

"Oh, that? That's just Skelly."

"I don't know anyone in Killjoy named Skelly. That's a strange name. Feel like I'd have remembered that'n."

Wells unzips the bag to reveal a poseable Halloween skeleton frozen in a plastic, perpetual scream. I roll my eyes. Meanwhile, Wells is grinning like an over-excited cartoon character.

"Wells! I thought that was real!"

"That's the point, dodo-bird." Wells strokes the skeleton's skull lovingly. "Hey, no, Skelly. You're real to *me*." He cackles maniacally and slaps his knee as he looks up at my disgusted face.

"You keep a fake piece 'a plastic in a real body bag?"

His voice is a little quieter as if he is worried about someone overhearing him. "It's a small town, Uma. Not a lotta people *die* here. Sometimes, I like to have him bagged on a rack so that if hospital staff walks by the door, I can look like I'm busy gettin' ready to start another exam. I get paid by the hour, you know. Don't wanna look *dispensable*. I got a mortgage on the lake house still."

"Oh, don't call it a lake house. You live in a trailer on the edge of the bayou. That thing's one hurricane away from being underwater. I've *seen* your place. It's like a glorified huntin' camp."

"With a *dock*!"

"Excuse me, a glorified huntin' camp… *with a dock*. Do you even have runnin' water out there?"

"Did you come here to find out what killed Carl, or did you come here to be hurtful and throw stones at the way I live? In case you have already forgotten, I'm doin' you a favor!"

"Sorry," I say with a laugh. "You're right."

"Words hurt, you know," he replies, followed by the giddy wiggle of his tush. Wells always acts like a stoned teenager or a Labradoodle puppy.

"Wells, thank you for the information. I will bring your jam out to you as soon as they let me back in my place again."

"Don't you dare forget to butter up Liv. I need you to do your best work."

"Oh, trust me, I *won't* forget."

He winces down at the body bag. "Eww."

"What?"

"You *really* thought you walked in on a professional pathologist eatin' gumbo out the crotch of a dead person?"

"After finding Carl face-down in a bloody pile of waffles, Wells, it wouldn't even be the weirdest thing I've seen this *week*."

"Oh, that reminds me! There was something odd with the blood work. Your vic's glucose levels were absolutely through the *roof*. I've actually never seen a human sustain numbers that high and live."

"Well... he didn't."

"Yeah, but he didn't die from the *diabetes*. He died from the brain trauma. But, I'm tellin' ya, with *those* sugar levels, if someone hadn't clubbed him in the skull, he would have probably gone into a full pancreatic shutdown soon."

I don't know what it means, but it feels significant.

"Those numbers were what I'd consider almost *suspiciously* high."

"Could it have been from the waffles?"

"Uma... he hadn't even taken a *bite* yet. The waffles were all intact. Nothin' super recent was makin' its way through his tract, either."

I make the bottom jaw of Skelly speak like it is my ventriloquist dummy. "Interestin'."

"Oh, and one more thing! Since we're friends and all -- and since I want that jam sooner rather'n later -- I should tell you..."

"Jus' spit it out, Wells. Don't be cryptic just 'cause you're bored. I got things to do today!"

He rolls his eyes. "I had a visitor this morning. About *Carl*. A woman came right to that door right there."

"And?"

"And... she was politely inquirin' about when I'd have a death certificate ready for Mr. Easterly."

"What? Already? He's barely even cold! Who was it?"

"Well, I asked if she was someone on behalf of the mortuary, eager to get a funeral underway, but she wasn't. She was an *ex-wife*."

"Was her name Lisa Slater? Curly brown hair, bigger-boned?"

"Well, she fits that description alright, but it wasn't Lisa. I know Lisa. She went to school with my third wife's daughter. Used to hang out at the house all the time. No, this was a Ms. Danielle Easterly. She said they recently divorced and that Carl's insurance company was requirin' it."

"What? What kind of insurance company? I didn't think they still owned a home together."

"They don't. Usually, the kind of insurance company that needs a death cert is a *life insurance* company."

It is mere seconds before I realize my mouth is hanging wide, staring at Wells with a look of shock that I'm sure makes me look like Edvar Munch's *The Scream*.

"Well, I'll be!" I finally say. "If she still has a life insurance policy on him…"

"Exactly. If that don't reek of motive, I don't know *what* does," Wells says. He shakes his head, and a grin spreads below his twisty mustache.

16

An old(er) woman passes me in the hallway of the *Fleur de Lis* Nursing Home as I scuttle to the front desk. She inches with a walker, focusing her eerie, walleyed stare toward a bathroom, face expressionless like one of those old-timey photographs where people used to pose morbidly with their deceased kin. The creepiest part isn't lookin' at her like she's a glimpse into my future... like I'm staring death right in its wrinkled face. No. The creepiest part is that I went to high school with her! She's three years younger'n me! Agnes, I think her name was. Or, technically, *is*, but I am tempted to use the *past* tense 'cause she looks like a vacant specter floatin' in search 'a someone to finally grant her a *release* from this realm.

"May I *help* you?" The receptionist has an attitude already.

I lean over the sign-in form toward her near a plexiglass partition. My drenched white curls drip onto the paper and clipboard below me.

"I'm here to see Melissa Owens, please."

"Ms. Owens is busy with our residents right now, ma'am." She blinks profusely and flashes me a phony smile that says, *Now go away, you old bat, before I make this place your home address.*

"I thought that might be the case," I say, rubbing my hands through my wet hair and flinging water drops like a drenched sheepdog all over the partition. I've learned through the years that the amount I annoy some staff often *directly correlates* to how quickly they resolve my issues, if for nothing more'n to get me outta their hair.

An orderly walks in, a male in all white, lookin' like St. Peter's bouncer at Heaven's pearly gates. A look of anger is affixed to his face, and his brown hand points out the door. "Ma'am, is that your Buick outside?"

I just stare at him for a long moment. "*Possibly.*"

"You can't park there. That's a *hydrant. And* one of your wheels is on the sidewalk!"

"I'll be outta here in a jiffy once this lady here points me to Melissa Owens."

A voice calls down the hall. "You're lookin' for Melissa?"

I turn and see another orderly. I nod and walk over to him. "Why, yes, as a matter of fact."

"Come. She's over here. Just got done giving a resident a sponge bath. Now she's setting up to scoop for the ice cream social today."

I look back at the soaked orderly at the door and the sheets of rain coming down behind him. "I'll only be a couple minutes. You won't even know I'm here! I'll be out in a flash," I lie.

Then, I look at the cranky broad behind the partition. "And if you're thinkin' of havin' me towed, I wouldn't bother. Thibodeaux Towing is the only service for miles. Andy Thibodeaux is not only a personal friend of mine, but he'd take at *least an hour* to get here with the volume of work he has. I'll be long gone by then."

It was a straight-up lie. My nose should be a foot long by now, at least. Andy hates my *guts*. He's had to haul my Buick away so many times I should have a special discounted rate with his family's tow yard by now! If these people called him and said it was a Buick Century, it'd fire Andy up to the point that he'd make haulin' my pile away his number one priority.

I smile smugly at the unhelpful lady at reception and then at the orderly at the door who doesn't exactly know what he should do. I head down the hall, darting into the room where the friendlier man just was. He waves me down one hallway and then another. This place is like a maze. I feel like I'm navigatin' catacombs.

"Melissa's in there," he says, holding the door to the recreation hall open for me. The floor is checkered, alternating cherry red and marbled white. Red, tufted pleather stools with faux chrome finish sit all around a crimson bar where a woman is placing buckets of ice cream down into a Baskin Robbins-style freezer well with a glass top. The place looks like a cheap ripoff of an old 50s diner, and it smells as old and decrepit as the residents are if Agnes was any indication of what the rest of them look like.

In the far corner, an ancient man is sittin' on a stool, starin' out the window at the pattering rain, probably waiting for the social to start, even though his sittin' alone seems like the very *antithesis* of the word social.

"Ms. Owens?" I ask, pressing my spotted hands to the cold glass, peering down at the flavors.

Melissa looks up, brown eyes studyin' me, lookin' for any spark of recognition.

"Ma'am, as I told Bartholomew over there, the social doesn't start for another forty-five minutes, so please… just… give me a few minutes to set up. I still have to prep all the sundae fixin's."

I laugh, though a little insulted. "Oh, I don't live here."

"Look, ma'am, I know it doesn't feel that way at first, but you'll make some friends before you know it, and soon this place'll really feel like a home."

"No," I laugh. "I mean, I'm parked outside. I came to see you. It's about Carl."

She bolts upright like her midsection was spring-loaded. Now I have her full attention.

"As you know, Carl has…" I try to think about how to delicately phrase that that piece of human garbage keeled over face-first into a pile of golden batter on my breakfast nook, "*passed.*"

I press my fingertips together and purse my lips, scrunchin' my face like I'm bein' electrically zapped by those sticky little TENS patches.

"I know you're busy settin' up for the social, and I'm parked… well, not exactly *legally,* so if I can ask you a couple of questions real quick, I'll be *right* outta your hair."

She looks at her watch, then back at me with a look that says she's ready to holler for an orderly at any moment. I should talk fast.

"I believe your husband, Clifford, came to my house the night before Carl was murdered. He 'bout gave me a doggone heart attack poundin' on my door that night."

She taps her foot, ice cream melting off the scoop in her hand in little droplets like opaque rain. "Was there a *question* in there somewhere?"

"I'm getting to that! Jeez! Everyone's so doggone *impatient.*"

"Well, I'm at work, and what my husband did—"

"Cliff mentioned that you just had a baby."

"…Yeah, so?"

"And he also said that the paternity of said child might be in question. Said it might be Carl's."

She grinds her teeth and stares at our seemingly catatonic third wheel, Bartholomew, in the corner.

"Correct me if I'm wrong, but it seems to me *that* might be enough reason for someone to wanna make a guy like Carl… *not exist anymore.*"

"And *who are you* exactly? I wasn't aware the cops had *senior* detectives."

"Let's not start hittin' below the belt, Mrs. Owens. We both know I don't work for the *cops.*"

"Then who are you?"

"I'm Jolene's mother. Uma Mae Blanchard."

A different expression crosses her face, one of pain and hilarity in equal measure.

"So you're that skank's mom? What a *prize* you raised." She seethes with sarcasm.

My eyes bulge. My volume rises. "I'd like you to rethink how you talk about my baby girl, Mrs. Owens."

"She was the other woman when he was with his ex, Danielle. Did you know that?"

"I had an inkling."

"Well, *she* wasn't the only one. Carl had a real… *charm* about him. In public, he was jovial and had this sort of easy charisma. But in *private*, he was suave. Real smooth. Could charm the pants off a bronze statue. Always had just the right thing to say to make you feel like you were the only girl in the world."

"Is that why you cheated on your husband with him?"

Her lips press together harder, lines wrinkling around her makeup-free mouth like rays on a hand-drawn sun. "It's why a *lot* of us were with him, I'm learning."

"Like Annie?"

"Annie, me, Jolene... his first wife, Lisa... hell, I'd heard he'd never even fully ended things with his *last wife*."

I groan and ask Bartholemew. "Good Lord, how did this man find the time?!"

Bartholemew doesn't reply. He just stares blankly. I follow his eyes out the window as lightning lights up the sky.

"Mrs. Owens, where was your husband after he left my place Wednesday night? Until, say, Thursday mornin', 'round four a.m.?"

"Like he told the sheriff, he was at *work*. The officers checked his alibi. He'd clocked in. People saw him at the front gate. Caught him on parking lot security cameras. He didn't leave til eight a.m. when his shift was over."

"And *you*? Mrs. Owens, where were *you*?"

"Ms. Blanchard, I have *four* young children. I was obviously at home with them. I got up around two-something to feed the baby and then again at seven-thirty. I was so tired that I passed out cold on the chair in the nursery while I was nursing. I don't get a lot of help around the house these days now that Cliff's been working nights."

Someone barges through the doors, a beefy man, probably six-foot-three. He is wearing dark jeans and cowboy boots, a solid color T-shirt tucked in behind a massive belt buckle. He stops mid-stride and looks at me strangely.

"Oh dear God." Melissa rubs her temple with her free hand and shoves the scoop back into a bucket of ice cream.

The man approaches cautiously. He hands Melissa the paper bag in his clutches. "Hey, babe. I... brought you... lunch. I figured you hadn't eaten."

"Thank you." She takes it from him, but I notice that they haven't once looked each other in the eyes since he came in.

"You the man who was beatin' down my door the other night?"

He studies me. "I've only beaten down one door this week, and it was because a coward I *used to* call my best friend was hiding behind it."

"Well, it was *my* house, not his. If it weren't tacky to do so, I'd shake your hand for givin' him that shiner. That man had it comin', if you ask me, what with all his alley-cattin' around."

"Are you... related to him?"

"*No*, thank God. Someone intervened in time." I point to Melissa. "She already told me your alibi's been confirmed, and havin' been a nursing mother myself, I am inclined to believe your story as well, Mrs. Owens."

160

"Don't get me wrong," Melissa says sternly. "I'm not upset that he's dead. He was playing me and a lot of *other* women for fools. What I did to Clifford was wrong. No one is more aware of that than I am, and we are working on ways to fix things so that maybe one day we can be stronger'n we *ever* were."

Cliff stifles a little bit of a smile as she says it.

"I *love* my husband. And I love my kids more than anything in this world. I'd *never* risk life in prison or a seat in Old Sparky for *any* man. As you can see, karma usually ends up doing that sorta thing *for* us if we're patient enough."

I look at Clifford. "How'd you find out about the affair?"

He takes a deep breath and looks into his wife's eyes. "She told me. Could've taken it to her grave, what with me bein' so focused on everything else in my life, but she didn't. She came clean, and she was woman enough to tell me. It was a wake-up call. Reminded me that If I don't pay attention to my family, I could lose 'em for good. I sure as heck don't want that." He shrugs. "Yeah, I was pissed at Carl. I considered him my best friend. Hell, I was gonna make him my kid's godfather. I can't tell you how many times he's had dinner with us or gone fishing with me and some of the other guys from the refinery. Carl was like *family* to me. I felt betrayed. But, once I punched him in his face and drove off, I felt… *horrible*. I felt, like, *hollow* inside. I never hit anyone before, and, yeah, in the *moment,* it was satisfying. But then reality set in. I had been neglecting my wife. For a *while*. I created this mess where I was drifting away while Carl was hornin' his way *in*. I should've never made her feel like she chould do better. *I take responsibility for that.*"

"Wow, Cliff." I nod.

I believe them. Both.

"One last quick question to satisfy my curiosity. Mind if I look at the soles of your shoes?"

They both look at me strangely.

"I believe you. I'm just tryin' to be thorough."

Cliff exposes the worn, smooth sole of his cowboy boot to me, and Melissa turns away and kicks her heel toward her scrub-clad butt. Neither one is anything close to the diamond pattern of the Vans.

"Well, thank you both for your time and honesty. I'll let you get back to your social. Looks like it's going to be a real hoot," I say, watching Bartholomew stare up at the ceiling tiles like they hold the answers to the world's mysteries. "I best git before Thibodeaux comes to haul my wheels away again."

I nod at them both and make my way out into the hall.

17

Back in Lagniappe's room 307, I stare at my corkboard. I write on another index card: **DANIELLE MARTIN.** Then, I cross through **MARTIN** and write **EASTERLY**.

DANIELLE ~~MARTIN~~ EASTERLY
Divorced. Occupation unknown. Carl's ex-wife. Divorced over cheating. Sniffing around at morgue for death certificate. Life insurance a possible motive. Alibi: Unknown

I pin it up. Then, I remove Clifford and Melissa's cards and toss them in the trash. I'm certain it isn't them. That leaves me with Danielle, Jolene, Lisa, and her husband, Frederick. I debate putting Jacoby on there just for good measure, but I can't bring myself to do it. Carl's parents are in town. Maybe they should be up there, too. If he were my son, I'd have wrung his neck a long time ago.

More'n anything, my daughter Jolene's card just keeps screamin' at me every time I look at it. She just has so much *motive*. Not to mention, opportunities galore bein' in the same house at the same time of the murder. With Moses not finding any forced entry yet, she's still my top suspect, unfortunately.

The only thing that brings me any relief is that I know she wouldn't be caught dead in a pair of those slip-on shoes that Eddie had on. Plus, those bloody footprints were large and her feet are small and dainty. Slip-ons *that* big would look like clown shoes on her!

Heck, now I'm almost wonderin' if I should put *Eddie* on the board. Redneck Cinderella may only be playin' innocent in all this, manufacturin' some wild alibi about scarin' someone away from a fire to hide the fact that he's still wearin' shoes that place him at the scene of the crime right in broad daylight.

No. I gotta stop. I'm spiralin', and everyone is startin' to look guilty. The whole town 'a Killjoy has me paranoid now.

After another twenty minutes of tryin' to find the email Cosmo sent me with the video files in my cluttered inbox, I give up and decide to do an internet search for Carl's second ex-wife, Danielle Easterly. After only a few minutes of diggin', I learn she's one of the head wranglers at the gator farm just outside Killjoy in a tiny municipality on Airline Highway called St. Rose. It's pretty much the shell of a town now, one comprised mostly of a small film studio, a couple 'a refineries, some warehouses, and a sprawlin' gator reserve and hatchery that rakes in a pretty penny from all the out-of-towners wantin' to see real live reptiles when they come to stay in Nawlins. Jokes on them, though. You can pretty much walk down to any body 'a water here in southern Louisiana and find a whole mess of 'em for *free*! You can get as up close and personal as you dare to get.

I scribble down the address of the gator farm so I can go there first thing in the morning when they open. After researchin' Danielle, I decide a break is in order. Cocodrie seems restless like he wants to go for a walk and stretch his li'l toothpick legs.

I open the door to my room at the inn. Rain is dumpin' down in sheets. Thunder rumbles in the distance, the thickest part of the storm still off to the west in the direction 'a Saint Amant. Fortunately, the one *appropriate* thing I packed in my suitcase was my slicker. I've been caught in some rough weather over the years on these cruises, so that was the *first* thing I stuffed in my bag, thank God.

I pull the rain slicker on over my neon Hawaiian shirt and tie the hood so tight that I look like that little orange fella off South Park who always sounds unintelligible.

"C'mon, Cocodrie," I mumble through the fabric as I tug him out to the walkway toward the elevator.

The metal box rattles and hums on our descent. The light above flashes, and the battered silver doors slide open.

Eddie is standin' there on the ground floor again, under the stairwell near the opening to the woods behind the hotel. I smile, and he returns it with one of his own.

"Well, well, well. Fancy seein' you here again, Uma."

"Afternoon, Eddie."

He offers me a cigarette from his pack. I wave it off. The last thing I need is to pick up the habit again.

"There was a deputy out here earlier lookin' for you. Took him up to your room, but you were out, it seems."

I'm puzzled. I already went down to the station to give my official statement. "What'd he want with me?"

"Well, I called him over here. Before this band of the storm really bore down, I saw someone messin' around back where that fire had been the other day. Figured it might be some little brat tryin' to light something else up. I called the cops, and they sent a deputy back there. The person took off the second they saw the squad car. I didn't get a good look at 'em, what with the dark cloud cover'n all."

Cocodrie wanders out in the rain, eyes narrowed suspiciously as he tries to get his bearings. Eddie flicks the cherry of his cigarette into a rippling puddle of runoff dribbling down from the overhang above us. It floats for a few seconds before the moisture finally gobbles it up.

"The deputy was back there looking to see if the arsonist left anything behind. Matches, lighters, kindling… et cetera."

"He find anything?"

"Nah," he takes another drag and then speaks as he's expelling the smoke. "Just a burned hammer."

"Where?!" I blurt a little too loudly.

"Right out there where the grass was all singed the other day, just off that concrete path where I found the shoes. Thing was just sitting right there. If it was a snake, it'd have bitten me." He shakes his head and looks out at the rain. "Ain't that somethin'? Perfectly good hammer... just... *wasted* like that."

My heart nearly skips three beats as the word *hammer* registers in my brain.

"The officer bagged it up and questioned a couple of the people in the hotel and then started askin' about you."

Cocodrie lets out a cranky yip at no one in particular, and it snaps me out of my confusing hodgepodge of thoughts. The fact that it was a hammer, of all things, *can't* be a coincidence. That's exactly what Wells thought Carl's murder weapon might be.

"Coco, you wanna go for a ride down to the station?" I ask the dog just as a flash of lightning lights the gray-black sky up to a pure sterling white.

Cocodrie gurgles a response of general displeasure, but since he seems incapable of getting excited these days, I'm still gon' take that as a 'Sure, Ma.'

18

"Good Lord, dat rain 'bout ran me into the ditch alongside Airline on the way here!" I shout to Clara, shakin' water off my slicker like a wet dog. Meanwhile, Cocodrie, the *actual* wet dog, stumbles around, bumps face-first into the leg of a chair in the waitin' room, and then takes a big gamble by hoppin' up on it like a rabbit. Fortunately, he sticks the landing. He perches in the plastic chair in a regal pose, lording over anything lower'n him. Water drips off him, puddlin' around his tan butt as he trembles with a strange air of sophistication and a general hoity-toity-ness I've not seen him exhibit in a while.

"You can't bring 'at dog in here, Uma."

"It's for emotional support," I say without missin' a beat, shruggin' off her protest. "Me for *him*, not the other way around. Heck, he wouldn't know how to emotionally support *me* even if there was a juicy T-bone in it for him."

She shakes her head, knowing full well I'm as stubborn as they come and that this'll all go a lot faster if she just ignores the damp, decaying creature.

"Amos came lookin' for ya at the Lagniappe. Said he couldn't find you." Clara holds up a neon sticky note on her fingertip. "So, thanks, I guess. You jus' saved me from havin' to call you in."

"Amos back there?"

"No, but Moses is. Hang on." Clara walks through the lobby, one that hasn't been updated since I was here reportin' that petty burglary back in the seventies on the day I met Harold. It's still all brown paneling and shorn dirt-brown carpet, not fit to wipe my shoes on.

Clara waltzes past a long rectangular fish tank with two giant black-and-orange Oscars in it. They float, bored and frownin', li'l flattened manatees pacing for their daily allotment of granulated food.

Clara raps on a door in the back and pokes her head in. "Sir, Blanchard's here. Want me to have her wait?"

Before Clara can get the last of the words out of her lipstick-slathered mouth, I dart around her, lettin' myself in. She throws her hands up in frustration. "Dang it, Uma. I told you to wait."

"Yeah, I know," I say. I know. I just don't care. I'll be seventy soon. My days are numbered, and nothin' burns me up more than younger people askin' me to *wait around* like I got all the time in the world.

Moses is at a workbench with a goose-necked black light. He holds a charred hammer delicately in his gloved fingers. The clawed end of the tool is lit up like a blue glowstick under the light.

"Oooooh. Pretty," I say.

The color reminds me of the bioluminescent water outside the Yuccatan, a place I'd be *on my way to tomorrow* had it not been for Carl *bitin' the big one* and leavin' us all with his doggone illicit affairs and entanglements!

"Dammit, Uma. You're not supposed to come back here," Moses groans, throwing his head back until the curls of his short afro mash into the divot between his shoulder blades.

"Moses, I'm not supposed to do a *lotta* things. I wasn't *supposed* to be born a month early. I wasn't *supposed* to light firecrackers in school. I wasn't *supposed* to lose the Prom Queen crown to cross-eyed *Ida Bates*. I wasn't *supposed* to get pregnant on the pill. And I *sure as heck* wasn't *supposed* to win the First Place Karaoke Champion Award on the Carnival Ignite with an *American Idol* runner-up on board, but guess who has a gold, plastic trophy on her kitchen shelf right next to her cookbooks?"

"I saw it when I was there processin' the scene," he grumbles. "I was *certain* it was a gag gift."

"Nope. The only gift I ever got was the God-given ability to sing *Sweet Dreams* better'n Annie Lennox herself."

"You got a trophy for singin' a *Eurythmics* song?"

"Oh, God, no, honey! I got that award for singing Warrant's *Cherry Pie*. Although, if I'm bein' honest, I think my sultry dance moves helped a bit." I wink.

Moses grimaces like he has straight rock salt on his tongue. Then, he shivers dramatically. "The mental image of you grindin' against an amplifier while singin' in your sixties is enough to make me upchuck and contaminate this hammer, Uma."

I stand on my tippy-toes and lean over the foldin' table between us with bagged items marked EVIDENCE.

"It's Carl's murder weapon, innit?" I ask.

"This is… for another case," he lies casually.

"Oh, that so? You got *two* vics with claw-shaped hack marks right through their parrot-all?"

"I think you meant *parietal*." He sighs heavily. "Dammit, Uma." He glances at me. "You talked to Wells, didn't you? I *knew* he was gonna be a weak link. That man has always carried a flame for you."

"Not me. Liv, apparently." I start to come around the table, inching closer to get a better look at the glowing item in his hands. "Don't blame Wells for foldin' like a house of cards. He's just a man. Men are weak when it comes to the fairer sex. If they *weren't*, we wouldn't be here right now talkin' 'bout the hammer that was buried inside Carl's noggin."

"Uma, please don't ever say the word 'sex' around me ever again. You're literally older'n my mother."

"By *two months*." I roll my eyes. "And our bodies don't stop havin' needs just because we get older."

"Stop."

"I'm still a hellcat." I wink at Clara.

"Stop! I will *find* something to arrest you for if you don't zip your lips, Uma." Moses turns to me, disgust and anger flashing in his walnut-colored eyes.

I sigh and smack my lips. "Wanna tell me why y'all were askin' around, lookin' for me at the Inn?"

"Amos was there to see if you knew anything about the fire in the woods. Plus, I know you've been snooping around, interrogating my witnesses, *exactly* like I axed you not to."

"It's *asked*, honey. Not *axed*. And I already done *told* you I was gonna help in an *unofficial* capacity. And I have. I got you some intel."

He perks up subtly, trying not to give away how much he needs everything I learned. "Alright then. Spill the beans, Uma."

"Well, seeing as though you were just *rude* to me… a little old defenseless woman, I don't know if I *should* help now."

"Well, how about this…" He points to a wall in the direction of his newly built holding cells. "You can either tell me what you know, or I'll make you up a cot in my nice new cell over there for interfering with an active investigation and obstructing justice. How'd you like a nice, firm, steel mattress instead of the springy one at the Lagniappe? Hmmm?"

I grind my dentures in frustration. Moses Cheramie really steams my grits sometimes.

"You're really going to lock up a sixty-eight-year-old woman like 'at? Think of the optics once I get out and blab to the reporters about how you treated little ol' me."

"Trunky Cordon is dating my niece. Half the anchors on Channel 8 are at my house weekly for poker night. If you think you are going to get anyone there to say one cross word about me, you're sorely mistaken. Don't overplay your hand, Uma."

I glance at Clara. "It was worth a shot."

"For the record," she says quietly, "I slept one off in there just before the ribbon-cutting event, and the cot actually wasn't half-bad. The next day, my sciatica pain was practically gone." She shrugs, unhelpful as usual with her need to chime in. "Just sayin'."

I glance up at Moses, unwilling to test the alleged therapeutic properties of the holding cell firsthand. "Wells said the murder weapon's curved. Said it seemed like the claw side of a hammer, which I'm assumin' is the one in your hand, one you found out there behind the hotel in the little burned patch in the woods."

"Stellar work, *Matlock*." Moses isn't impressed. His sarcasm don't bother me one bit, though, because I'm not finished.

"The hammer was found in a spot off the main walkin' path where Eddie Pickles, the guy that runs the hotel, found himself a checkered pair of Vans slip-on shoes the other night. Cinderella said they happened to fit. Here, Eddie thought it was his lucky day gettin' himself a free pair of sixty-dollar *Ridgemont High* knock-around shoes. Meanwhile, he's most likely been wearin' the shoes our killer tracked blood all over my kitchen's laminate with. I recognized the strange little diamond-shaped tread pattern immediately when I saw it. I'll bet you if you hosed those puppies down with that Luminol and put those slip-ons under this black light, they'd dang-near blind you."

"You sure about that?"

"I don't think it takes a genius to figure out whoever was out there havin' themselves a little impromptu bonfire was destroyin' evidence. Probably just got interrupted before they could finish the job, and they took off."

Moses places the hammer in a bag and seals it. He marks it with some scribbles I can't quite read and mumbles, "That all?"

I laugh. "Nope. I paid Melissa Owens a visit today at the old folks' home down there on Mariposa. She was there doin' a little ice cream social for all those dusty old farts. Her hubby, Cliff, stopped by while I was there, so I got myself a lucky little *two-for-one* break. The Cliff's notes -- *pun intended* -- are that Clifford punched Carl out because he found out the scuzz-ball had been havin' an affair with his wife, Melissa. Cliff said after that, he went straight to work while Melissa was at home gettin' up all through the night breastfeedin' the newborn -- *who may or may not be Carl's*. Now, as someone who has breastfed five children before—"

"Ugh, Uma, I don't want to hear about your breasts or anything else on your body." Moses plugs his ears and shakes the thought out of his head.

"As someone who's had newborns," I say louder, ignoring his childish behavior, "I can't imagine she could watch all four of her kids, *and* go beat a man to death with a hammer, then take it out to the woods to burn the evidence and make it back home in time for another feeding, *and* still go do a full day at work without ever bein' noticed. That just seems dang-near impossible."

"Agreed," Clara says from the doorway. Moses and I look up at her with matching expressions that say, *"You're still here? Don't you have something better to do?"*

I turn back to Cheramie. "Moses, tell me about the hammer."

He sighs again, the sound heavy with reluctance. "Steel, rip-claw framing hammer. Perforated yellow-and-black anti-vibe grip."

"Brand?"

"Unsure. The insignia's not a common logo. Hopin' it's some kinda local up-and-coming brand or something. Clara's gonna start checking the databases to find a match. Maybe we'll get lucky, and it'll be only carried a few places around here."

"Prints?"

"No prints. The handle was too burned. Heat damages the oils when you roast something like a hot dog. Amos thought he got one partial, but so far, it hasn't matched anything in our databases." He lugs the bag up in the air in front of me, and I get a good look at the logo, a 'B' inside a crescent moon. "As you just saw, even though it was burned, the Luminol glowed up that claw end. I'll have the lab test it to confirm that the DNA comes back a positive match for Easterly."

"Speaking of Carl, did you hear the hot gossip from Wells about the missus?"

He looks at me, confused. "No."

"Well, technically, it was *one* of the exes. I tell ya, hearin' about that boy's sex life straight-up exhausts me."

"What's your point, Uma?"

"Well, Wellsy said Carl's most recent ex-wife came sniffin' around the morgue today. She was apparently askin' if Wells had issued a *death certificate* yet... for the *insurance company*. As in *life* insurance, most likely. Seems like she may have had a policy out on Carl. And, you know, him being dead now, that just might land her a nice, fat payday."

"I think divorce usually nullifies those, but I'll speak to Wells and confirm. If it's an active policy with her as a beneficiary, that could very well be motive."

"That's what I thought, too!" I smile. "See? It pays to have me around, doesn't it? I help *you* with the case, and you help *me* get my butt on that five-day cruise ship to the Yucatan."

He laughs and shakes his head. "Uma, you are somethin' else." He stares at the floor for a moment. "I'll start working on all these reports. Danielle had an alibi, but I'll send Amos to pay her another visit and see what he can find out about the insurance stuff."

"She probably won't be home," Clara volunteers. "She never is anymore. She's probably gonna be up there at the club."

"Which one?" Moses says, clicking off the black light.

"The Honky Cat."

It sounds less like a nightclub and more like the perfect way to describe Clara Torelli's voice. She sounds like a sick Tabby trying to meow in the middle of a hairball hack.

"She's been up 'ere three or four times a week since their divorce. I think she's tryin' to find hubby number three."

"What a pair they must have made. Pfft. The Honky Cat? Great place to find Prince Charming," I mutter with an eye roll.

"Hey, it's *hard* dating here in Killjoy, Uma," Clara says defensively.

I look at Moses. "You said Danielle had an alibi?"

"She did."

"Ironclad?"

Moses looks away. "I can't discuss specifics with you. It's... *sensitive*."

"Intriguin'." Now, I *need* to know what that means a *thousand* times more.

"Even though she was able to prove *her* whereabouts, that opens this up to a potential murder-for-hire scenario now. Leave her alone, Uma. I assure you, we'll get to the bottom of the insurance stuff." He fidgets with the corner of one of the evidence bags. "You found anything else that might be of use, Sherlock?"

"As a matter of fact, I did. Word on the street's that Lisa, Carl's *first* ex-wife, and her husband, Frederick Slater, might need to be put under the magnifyin' glass, too. Everyone 'round Killjoy's been sayin' Lisa still had a pretty substantial... *thing* for Carl."

I shudder at the thought of anyone findin' that man attractive, much less a whole gaggle of eligible Killjoy women, one of which has a direct genetic link to me.

"People are makin' it sound like if he'd have even *hinted* at wantin' Lisa back, she'd have pushed Freddy and the kids to the curb in a second. Carl's apparently been stringin' her along in his messages."

"Messages?"

"That's the other thing I came here for. Jolene said Payzlee was playin' with the iPad this morning and accidentally pulled up some sorta hub where you can see the whole family plan's messages on some cloud thingy. Anything they wrote on any of the connected devices shows up on it, apparently. She found out about Carl's second phone. It apparently has a Hindu design on it. Jacoby thinks it might be *Shiva*."

"Good Lord, Uma. Maybe I should fire Amos and hire you."

I chuckle proudly. "I told you that years ago when Harold handed you the torch." I nod at him and change the subject. "You found that second phone yet? Was it on him when he was brought to the morgue?"

"No. It wasn't in his personal effects, and Wells didn't mention one in his reports."

I dig into my alligator-skin handbag and produce Payzlee's iPad, handing it over to Moses. "I read through the messages this afternoon at lunch while I was down at *Cooter's* eatin' my red beans and rice. You can have it. I didn't find too much of use. Seems he used it to talk to a few women on a buncha different datin' sites. I imagine it was a sort of spray-and-pray situation, a real numbers game. But when he hooked a fool like Annie Waghorn, he'd sometimes copy-and-paste his little love letters from one woman to the next and change almost nothin'. Called everyone 'Babydoll' or 'Sugar,' probably 'cause it was impossible to keep their names straight. Boy got *around*."

"Oh, I'm *aware*," Moses says, hoisting the iPad like a drink at a table. "Thank you. We will do a full forensic search of it."

"The only thing I really gleaned from the letters is that there was more *give* than *take* as far as Lisa Slater was concerned. Carl seemed to give her less attention than any of the others. My guess is that her throwin' herself at him was a turn-off. Maybe he liked the thrill of the hunt more than the kill. But then again, if she found out how many other women Carl was actually givin' the time-a-day to, that could cause enough of a jealous spark to fuel a murder, I'd reckon."

"Great work, Colombo," Moses teases.

"Oh… one last question before I git."

"What's that?"

"What's the shoe size of the print you found in the kitchen?"

"Men's size ten. Why?"

"Because when I go back to the Lagniappe, I'll ask Eddie what the size is of the ones he found out there by the fire. I'll call you when I get an answer. Your number still 9-1-1?"

"No, Uma. Let me do it. I'd rather you not. If they *are* the right size, I don't want him gettin' panicked and potentially destroyin' them just so he doesn't get wrapped up in all this. People see all these shows on the TV nowadays, and this guy might think he's gonna do time for evidence tamperin' or something. I'd rather it be me so I can collect 'em and have a proper chain of custody when we hand everything over to the DA."

"Alright. Fine."

"You need a ride back to the hotel?"

"No, I've got the Buick."

"Oh, Lord. God help us all," Clara's gravelly voice says as she makes the sign of the cross.

A few minutes later, Cocodrie and I are back in the parkin' lot, and I'm feelin' hopeful that if tomorrow goes well, I might still be able to salvage my cruise.

When I reach my vehicle, I see something flapping wild in the tropical depression winds against my windshield. It buzzes against the glass like a fluttering hummingbird's wing. I rip it out from underneath the wiper. It's short, written ransom-style from letters cut out of newspaper headlines.

It just says:

IT WAS DANIELLE.

I look left and right, scanning the block for another car or bike or human who might've placed this thing on my Buick.

But I don't see a soul. Just the wind smacking around overgrown foliage as the incoming storm thrashes trees and wobbles phone lines.

I get in, toss the suspicious message onto my dashboard, and start the car. I whip out of my parking spot so fast that I give one of the impounded vehicles behind me a little *love tap* on its bumper. As I pull away, I jump the curb, one that has a rut in it where someone has apparently jumped it in the past.

I ignore the 'No Turn on Red' sign and take a right onto the highway, deep in thought about the ransom-style confession.

Does someone know I'm digging into this case, and they want to anonymously help? Or is it a ruse to thwart me and throw me off a scent I'm on?

Either way, I think it's time I go down to The Honky Cat for a little visit…

19

There aren't any spots available in the lot, so I make my own parkin' space in the grass beside the building. Steam oozes through the cracks in the Buick's hood, bathed in the sickly yellow light from a neon sign that reads: *The Honky Cat*. The rain has subsided for a bit, but the wind is kickin' now, rattling loose trash and long-dead leaves along the busted brick base of the building. I scuttle up to the muscular guy standin' against the wall next to the front door.

"'Scuse me, young man. Is there a cover charge to get in?" I ask, hoping I don't have to whip out my coin purse and start countin' out discontinued pennies just to see if my youngest daughter's dead fiancee's former wife is here.

Wow, what a convoluted mouthful *that'd* be to say aloud.

"No, I don't think so."

"You don't think so? Or *there isn't?*"

He shrugs his beefy shoulders, ones covered in a tight black T-shirt.

"Ain't you the bouncer?"

He laughs and shakes his head. "Just a patron. I'm waitin' on someone."

I grab one of his rock-hard biceps and squeeze. He watches me with a look of shock and disbelief. "You should switch to tank tops. Can't be walkin' around Louisiana with *concealed weapons* like that 'less you got a permit."

The man turns three shades of pink beneath the buzzing yellow neons as he realizes I'm givin' him a compliment. "I'll keep that in mind, ma'am."

"Say, handsome," I can't help myself from flirtin' even though he's probably Jolene's age and has enough muscles to snap my brittle spine like a twig, "You seen a woman named Danielle in 'ere?"

"Curly hair? Part Latina? Kinda a bigger gal?"

"Yep. I think that's the one."

"She usually hangs out by the back door, the one that leads out to the smoker's area. You might try there."

"Thank you," I say, fightin' the urge to wink.

I enter the building, feelin' the thump of the bass travel up through my Mary Janes, permeatin' my tibias as I make my way through all the people. The bar is almost vibratin' with desperation. The music is cranked up to an absolutely migraine-inducin' level. Back in my day, bars were never this loud. Jukeboxes, sure as heck, were never turned up to these kinda cochlea-damagin' volumes.

I order a mojito from the bar so I can walk around with something and blend in a little. I'm sure I stick out like a sore thumb. I'm probably a good twenty years older'n anyone here.

The bartender makes my drink in a dirty glass and slides it across the counter.

"I take it you don't need to card me?" I joke.

He barely cracks a smile.

"What gave me away? Was it the white hair?"

He doesn't respond. He just takes my twenty and makes me change, some of which I stuff in a tip jar, even though he didn't even bother to humor me.

I sip my beverage, meanderin' through the throng of people, some playin' billiards, some dancin', some with their hands down the pants of the person they're next to. I try not to gawk.

I make my way over toward a door to a walled-in outdoor smokin' area with a warnin' near the window about how Louisiana doesn't allow smokin' inside its establishments.

I walk through, listening to the *whoosh* of wind that's picked up even more in the last few minutes. It's gotta be fifteen, twenty miles an hour right now, thrashin' everything. I wouldn't be surprised if we have power outages in the parish tonight. I only hope it doesn't flood.

So much of southern Louisiana sits in a doggone *bowl* surrounded by levees unfit for Don McLean to sing about.

A lone woman is leanin' against the wooden privacy wall of nailed-together pallets lined with string lights. She is tryin' her best to light a cigarette, but thanks to the wind, she seems to be failin' miserably. I recognize her almost instantly, though she's gained a lotta weight since she used to be a Martin.

"Danielle Easterly?" I step toward her. She stares at me distrustfully. I cup my age-spotted hands around the end of her smoke to help her light it. She sucks hard as she flicks the stubborn flame back on until a bright red cherry forms at the end. I lower my hands with a smile, watchin' the gray line of smoke rip straight into the ether from the force of the wind.

"Oh my. Uma Blanchard." She shakes her head. "I ain't seen you in a dog's age. Not since, what, the auditions a few years ago?"

"I got robbed, I tell ya. My Supertramp was on *point* that day. I even did air-harmonica for those judges an' it didn't move the needle for them one bit."

"Oh my God. That's right. *Take the Long Way Home.* Can't believe I forgot that. Hey, at least you made the promo on TV."

"I think that was jus' to show the diversity of the candidates." I look up at the swingin' trees above us, partly in awe of their beauty as they sway, partly in fear 'cause

I've seen so many crack and fall through the years in storms like these.

"What brings you to this run-down hole, Uma?" She blows out a mouthful of smoke that gets vacuumed away the second it leaves her lips.

"*You*, actually." I turn back to her. "I'm sure you're well aware my daughter was Carl's newest flavor of the week."

"Yep." She laughs, diggin' her shoulder back into the pallet wall like a bear tryin' to itch itself on its zoo enclosure. "The big day was gon' be tomorrow, right?"

I nod, wondering how my daughter, Jolene, is holdin' up on the eve of what was s'posed to be her most special night.

"I guess I'm sorry for your loss... or whatever," Danielle says half-heartedly.

"Well, it's no real secret. I wasn't a big fan of the big buffoon myself. I only spent a few weeks livin' with him. I can't imagine what you must have gone through after bein' with him for the better part of a decade."

She nods, sharing a sort of kindred affinity for me that sorta even resembles respect.

"Where were you the night he died?" I ask blatantly. Life is short. Death's clock is tickin' louder'n it ever has. I might as well just get to the point.

She takes another drag of her cigarette and smiles. "I was... bein' intimate with someone."

"Does he have a name?"

"*She*. And, yes, she does. But it don't matter. Cheramie cleared me. I gave him doorbell footage showing us arriving back at her place after The Honky Cat closed. We never left. Not until work the next day."

"I see."

"She rocked my world."

"Thanks, but I don't quite need *that* much information." I sigh, nervous to broach the next accusation. "The coroner said you came 'round askin' for his death certificate today."

"Sure did." She says it so carefree like Carl never meant anything to her. Maybe she's jaded by his actions, protectin' her heart from further trauma by pretendin' she never really cared for the man. "When I caught him cheating for the thousandth time… with your *daughter*, no less… I filed for divorce. He was so broke at the time and owed me so much money. The judge ordered him to keep life insurance on himself and make me the beneficiary 'til he paid me back for all the debt he'd put me in. That way, if something like this ever happened, I wouldn't be left in the cold."

"I didn't even know a judge could do that. I thought divorce nullified a life insurance policy on an ex."

"Sometimes, but not always. In this case, the judge was a woman, and I take it she had been burned by some of the Carls of the world, too. She threw the book at him. That's probably why he was livin' with you and not in some apartment with Jolene. The dumb fool had absolutely ruined his credit."

"I see."

She takes another drag and laughs it out in small puffs like a tiny locomotive. "I'm not sad he's dead, Uma."

"Well, that makes *two* of us, if I'm bein' honest."

"I wanted him dead. He's worth more to me *in* the ground than he *ever* was above it, the mouth-breathin' idiot."

I chuckle at the morbid honesty, grateful my youngest can't hear me. It'd break her heart to know how everyone felt about the guy she was set to wed.

"Between you, me, and this Marlboro," she flashes a half-smile and twists the filter in her fingers, watching the wind ignite the cherry a bright fire-red, "I *tried* to kill him."

I'm stunned by her confession, unsure of what to say or do. I spent all this time lookin' for the perpetrator and absolutely no time at all thinkin' about what I'd do if I *found* the person responsible.

"Not this week, mind you. But over the last couple of months." She chuckles. "It's messed up, I know, but when we were together, sex wasn't the only thing he seemed to have no self-control over. The man's diabetes was *unreal*. Doctors told him he was on a path to losin' his feet or eyes or that he could flat-out die if he didn't watch his sugar intake closer. Of course, Carl didn't heed that advice one bit. Went to the buffet afterward every time and stuffed his face like blood sugar wasn't even a thing."

She laughs and looks up at the Louisiana state flag flappin' wild above us on a pole.

"When we were married, Uma, I *tried* to keep him in check. I nagged. I meal-prepped. Hell, I even taught him how a *pancreas* works. We even made a little drawing of it when his started to fail. Kept it on the fridge. Gave it a name so he'd start thinking of it as something he needed to try to save. Didn't do one lick of good."

I soak in every word of her story. It aligns perfectly with how I saw the man eat despite Jolene's flippant mentions of him havin' diabetes.

"Doctors had him on insulin after a while, but he was real hit-and-miss at using it. Carl was lazy as all get-out, and with his illness, it was like he had an actual death wish or somethin'. Maybe he was tryin' to punish himself for all the messed up stuff he did to women over the years." She shrugs. "When we divorced, he had free reign. Every time I came to his job to drop off more of his things, he was downin' soda or stuffin' sugary food in his face."

I shift uncomfortably, wonderin' what this has to do with her tryin' a kill him. But I don't have to wait long.

"So once that judge forced him to get the life insurance policy, I started anonymously sendin' him a dozen donuts every other day at the refinery, knowing that he wouldn't have the self-control to resist 'em. I had a standin' order and a prepaid credit card on file. I think he thought they were from one of his mistresses if I'm honest."

She laughs again, this time with a hint of sadness in it, like she's remembering a fonder memory.

"Didn't work though. Months went by, and he packed on a ton of weight, but nothin' ever seemed to happen. All it did was slowly bleed my bank account dry. The guy was indestructible. Or... so I thought." She stares at me for a moment, the chartreuse glow of the neon lights glinting in her watery eyes. "Seems like someone was kind enough to save me another nine months of bakery bills by cuttin' to the chase."

"It would appear so."

She smiles again. "Sure wish I knew who it was. I'd send 'em a *thank you* card with a picture of me standin' in front of the house I'm about to pay off."

As much venom as she's got stored for a dead man, one prepped for his last time bein' the center of every Killjoy woman's attention tomorrow, I believe her. Sure, she wanted him dead, but Danielle's too patient for such a violent demise. Sending him donuts for *months*? That's so passive and drawn-out. That's not the kinda behavior I'd expect from someone with the guts to hit him in the back of his bald head with a hammer.

20

This morning, after crossin' Danielle off my list of suspects and wolfin' down a pile of breakfast beignets, I load up Cocodrie and make the forty-five-minute trek over to the St. Rose Gator Preserve. Two iron gates greet me at the beginning of a long dirt path that snakes through swampy wetlands and tufts of tall grass. In a place like this, the mosquitoes usually outnumber humans ten thousand to one.

I curl down the path, weaving my way to the parking lot. Despite how tucked back into the middle of nowhere this place is, there's a *ton* of cars here. I drive down a long row of vehicles parked along a rickety shack. Each car has an out-of-town plate. Texas. Oklahoma. New Mexico.

Heck, there's even one from Wyoming in the lot with the little brown buckin' bronco on it.

I park near a homemade wooden sign for the visitor's center etched into a slab of cypress. Then, I wake Cocodrie from his slumbers. Slumbers, in which he'd been passin' noxious gas so bad I had to roll down a window. The sewage treatment plant along the way had a *far* better smell than my interior does right now.

Cocodrie sneezes and waddles toward the steps of the visitor center, stoppin' to growl at an intimidatin' rock along the way. He bares what's left of his rancid teeth, and I tug him across the threshold inside.

The visitor's center is filled with gator-themed trinkets, shirts, alligator back-scratchers, and toys. It opens up into another room full 'a general Cajun tourist wares: profane bottles of hot sauce, plastic jars of comically-named spice mixes, snarky T-shirts, children's books in Cajun-French, pelican snow globes, and humorous shot glasses.

I waltz up to the front desk, hearin' the click of my Chihuahua's overgrown nails on the floor (the vets'll no longer touch 'em on account of how violent he gets. I sure as *hell* am not gon' do it myself and get my face gnawed off.)

"Ma'am, you can't have your dog in here. I'm so sorry." The lady at the front desk has a southern twang that'd make Dolly Parton's eyes bulge.

"Oh, it's alright. He's an emotional support animal," I lie again and then talk quickly to change the subject. "Is Lisa Slater here today?"

The woman stares at me with an odd look, suddenly takin' in my attire. I'm donnin' a sequinned black formal gown, one I planned to wear to the Captain's Dinner on the cruise ship I was supposed to board this afternoon. I'm hopin' that she doesn't notice the powdered sugar across the neckline that I can't seem to get out without a wet washrag. (Those beignets are delicious, but I challenge anyone to eat an order of 'em without wearin' any of the sugar. *It simply can't be done!*)

I realize I must stand out like a goth kid at a rave wearin' this glittery dress and stubby satin heels, but what's anyone expect me to wear? I only have what's in my suitcase.

"If you're wonderin' 'bout my attire, I'm headin' to a funeral soon."

"Whose? Sigfried and Roy?"

I chuckle. I have to admit, that comment was a little funny.

"Yes, I'll admit this is a little… *festive*… for a funeral, but desperate times call for desperate measures, sweetheart."

"Bless your heart…" she coos sweetly, but down south, those are fightin' words. She might as well have just told me outright she thinks I'm touched in the head. "Mrs. Slater is here, but I'm afraid she's busy. Unfortunately, she's got to leave in a bit."

I point to my dress, one reflectin' small dots of light onto her face. "I know she does, ma'am. I'm attending the same funeral. Can you just get on an intercom or a walkie and have her come here, please? Thanks so much!" I smile and hope it works to be a little pushy. Sometimes it does.

I don't know if it's my age or the sugar-sweetness in my tone that makes people fold like a house of cards, but whatever it is, it works more often than not.

"No," she says firmly.

Dang. Well, it was worth a shot.

"I'm sorry, hun. We don't have an intercom to summon her, but even if we did, she's busy. If you'd like to purchase a ticket to walk the preserve with our other guide, that'll be five dollars. Otherwise, you're free to peruse the gift shop to your heart's content." She motions to the shop I'm already standin' in. "Then again, if you're goin' to the same funeral, you could always talk to her there."

I sure could, but she'll be in front of a lotta grievin' people. I won't be able to get an accurate read on the woman's emotions. Or Freddy's, for that matter.

For a moment, I debate my next move. In my mind, all signs point to Carl's killer being Lisa or Freddy at this point. Lisa has been cast aside for woman after woman… *after woman*… and Freddy's been watchin' his wife fawn over this uncaring, disloyal piece of trash for decades. Frankly, they both have motive. If I could just talk to either of them in private…

"Gimme a ticket for the preserve. What was it you said? Five bucks?"

"Yes, ma'am. Five dollars." She points to Cocodrie. "But your puppy absolutely can't go. I'm afraid I have to be firm 'bout that."

"First of all, he's about fifteen years away from bein' considered a *puppy*. Second, if you're worried about a gator snappin' him up, you can rest easy. If Cocodrie and an alligator were to go at it, my money'd be on that Chihuahua all day."

"I'm afraid I can't let that little thing go through those doors."

"Okay," I trade the ticket in her hand for a wrinkled fiver and wrap his leash around a nearby clothin' rack. "I'll only be a minute!"

"Ma'am, I can't…!"

"Don't let any kids near him! He looks cute an' cuddly, but he ain't in the slightest," I holler over my shoulder. Before she can say another word in protest, I bolt through the back door marked 'Gator Sanctuary.'

"Miss!" She crows again, but I close the door behind me and scurry down the wooden plank path, black heels clackin' against the boards as I make my way past several open, swampy pits full 'a reptiles. Some are up on the banks, blobbed out like fat tourists tryin' to dry out on the dirt in between the rainy tropical storm bands. Others sit in the murk, evil eyes followin' me like a tasty treat.

"Lisa? Freddy?" I holler their names as I make my way to an observatory perched at the edge of a dock that juts out over the water. The waterline is high. I imagine if the storm lets loose again, after about another half an hour of rain, these gators'll be able to crawl up on the main plank path I'm on!

I hear a woman up ahead dishin' out factoids about the American alligator and the differences between it and its crocodile and caiman cousins. I dart down another row of boards once the path splits off in two directions. I head down around another black lake full 'a soakin' ten-foot gators.

I scan the area and see a woman that matches how Jolene once described Lisa. Jacoby was a little more flatterin' in his stories, but then again, she *is* his mother.

"Lisa Slater?" I ask, approachin' as the woman slings raw chicken quarters at the alligators in yet another stale, mosquito-infested pond. One of the animals, which has to be at least twelve feet long, catches a hunk of fowl in its gaping maw like a Labrador retriever and chomps down with an awe-inspirin' force. He reminds me of my dog but without all the hot spots and hair.

"Can I *help* you? The tour guide is back down that way." The woman seems perturbed at my interruption. She reaches into her plastic five-gallon bucket and whizzes another hunk 'a meat at a second gator. It lands in the mud by his face, and he just stares for a moment, unmoving. It isn't until the first alligator threatens to take it that his jaw snaps open, and an ungodly warning hiss emits from the back of his throat.

"Good Lord!" I focus my attention back on Lisa. "I'm Uma Blanchard."

The woman's eyes roll with disgust. "Oh, I see. You raised that little harlot, *Jolene*, didn't you?" She drags the name out of her mouth like it's a curse word she's savorin'.

"I'd appreciate it if you didn't call my daughter that," I say, imagining myself charging across the plank walkway and shovin' this woman right into her own gator pit for callin' my kin such a thing. Jacoby is already buryin' one parent today, and at this moment, I dream of making him a full-blown orphan.

But, instead, I remain composed.

"Or what? Huh?" She waggles a chicken leg at me, and the loose flap of skin clinging to it dangles limply. "*You* raised a daughter with loose morals who takes what ain't hers. Then, you have the *nerve* to come here to *my* job to… what… *harass* me?"

"I'm not here to harass you, so… just save that salmonella for the reptiles."

She hurls the hunk of chicken in her hand into the pit. The slow gator leaps into action again, snarlin' until the other retreats into the green-brown water.

"I'm jus' here to ask you a few questions. Ones an innocent person wouldn't *usually* be so defensive over."

"What're you gonna ask that the sheriff hasn't?"

"Well," she's got me there. I actually don't know what she's already told Moses. "Let's start with you tellin' me where you *allegedly* were the night of Carl's murder."

"Ma'am, we had a *casualty* that day. Maggie, one of our senior alligators, passed away. That alligator was old.

She'd been sick for a while, but she died that night at the end of my shift," she chucks another wad of slimy, pink meat into the enclosure. "Fred and I got a call once the vet did his autopsy, and we came back. Once we found out what the cause of death was, we got the okay to process her."

"What do you mean *process* her?"

"When we get the okay from the vet, we skin 'em and sell the meat to local restaurants. We process the hides for the footwear companies we have contracts with. It's time-sensitive, and every bit we can sell helps us with the cost of upkeep in this place." She waves a dripping chicken breast in my direction. "Gators ain't cheap. Hell, these guys eat a lot better'n I do half the time!"

"You said 'we.' Does Freddy help?"

"No, I pretty much do all the processing. Fred just helps me get 'em up on the hoist. That night, after we got Maggie up, he stayed and worked on the new breeding box the owners contracted him for. Workin' at night 'round here is nice because the bats are taking care of the mosquitoes, and the heat ain't as sweltering and muggy."

Working at this preserve sounded like my nightmare job. Mosquitoes, bats, alligators, mud, humidity, and heat? No, thank you!

"What time did y'all get here to start processin' Maggie?"

"As I told Cheramie, I got the call to come back around 11:30. Didn't get done until around four a.m."

Oh, Lord! That's when Carl was killed! This alibi still doesn't clear her or Freddy…

"Where'd you go after that?"

She flings another wad of meat like a frisbee. Two baby gators come rushin' out of some tropical sago palms toward it, scaring the daylights out of me as they appear from practically nowhere. They were hidden in plain site all this time, still as a rock!

"Look, Uma, if I wanted Carl dead, which I *didn't*, I have enough tools in the back to make him into free gator food. I'm surrounded by four hundred pounds of hungry, carnivorous dinosaur descendants who would literally eat that man for breakfast. There wouldn't have been a body. The man would have just vanished without a trace, leaving nothing but a letter sayin' he'd run off with another woman."

Hmmm, she's got a point. And if Fred had access to all that stuff too, it don't make much sense to drive forty-some miles to go crack the man's head like an egg in my breakfast nook.

"Do you know anyone else who might've wanted to do this to Carl?"

The woman bursts into a full-blown sob, and I see her reflexively try to wipe her eye with a hand covered in syrupy chicken blood. She decides against it at the last second. I watch her shudder. Her cries turn into a wail, and she violently dumps the whole rest of the bucket of chicken parts into the pit at once with a growl. It splatters against the muddy bank, and more gators come out of nowhere in a big free-for-all feedin' frenzy, violently snappin' and chompin'.

Lisa hurls the slick bucket toward a small structure. The bucket hits with a plastic *thud*. She howls out in anger. A moment later, a man crawls out onto the mud. It is only then that I realize he's been in one of the gator enclosures this entire time!

"What?!" He's livid, totally unfazed by the bloodthirsty gators within striking distance. He stares up at Lisa from the muddy pond bank. "What are you doin'?! I'm in there trying to screw on hinges, and you scare me half to death!"

She looks away, unwilling to let him see how hard she's crying.

"Oh God, not again! How much are you going to mourn for this loser?!" He tosses his mud-slathered screw gun up onto the platform we are on. It clatters against the wood. He climbs a rickety four-rung ladder near her feet and wipes the muck from his hands off onto his filthy ribbed tank top, one that's unsalvageable from the amount of grime caked on it.

He looks at me and points with ferocity at Lisa. "Please tell me she ain't crying over Carl again!"

I don't say anything. I'm still just *stunned* that he was just working in reach of so many alligators this whole time!

"Screw this!" He stomps back toward the gift shop, U-turns, and retrieves his dirty screw gun and a mud-caked tool bag.

"Wait, Freddy, I'm sorry," Lisa wails, grabbing his muddy arm with her chicken-drenched fingers. Suddenly, I am in need of five back-to-back showers after seeing the hygiene of these two.

But the name she shouted surprises me.

It's Freddy! I hadn't even realized I could talk to them both! It never occurred to me that he might be here.

As Freddy stomps off, he flips his wife the bird, but I can't really bother to be shocked by it because my eyes are focused on the mud-soaked prints his Timberland boots leave behind. While having different shoes on right now doesn't rule him out, the fact that he would've allegedly been leavin' here and goin' straight to my house and changin' into flashy little Vans just to end Carl's life feels like a long shot.

Furious, Lisa kicks the braces for an overhead observation deck, one where you could see the whole preserve if you went up on it. I notice that she's wearin' boots, too. Worn ones with a similar tread to Freddy's, probably ones everyone who works here has to wear so's they can navigate the muddy terrain with these prehistoric-lookin' monsters.

"I'm sorry to have bothered you, Lisa," I say quietly so she doesn't get the urge to kick *me* next. "I s'pose I'll be seein' you at the funeral this afternoon?"

She nods solemnly and stares in the direction of the door Frederick just exploded through in his fit of rage. Then, she finally speaks, face twisted in a furious snarl. "I really loved him, you know."

"*Carl?*" I ask with an air of incredulity, still surprised that anyone could with all his alley-cattin' around. Before she speaks, I already know the answer. Everyone in town that I talked to confirmed it, but it was her reluctance to chase her *current* husband because she was too busy mournin' her *past* one that just cinched the deal.

Lisa starts to speak, but it seems like she can't breathe through all the cryin'. It looks like she's about to faint on the spot. "I never... stopped... lovin' that man."

I look away and watch a baby alligator snap through a chicken thigh like a dried twig, all the while starin' at me with its dead-lookin' eyes. Then, I realize that I'd rather watch Lisa cry over my daughter's decomposin' fiancee. It's somehow *slightly* less unsettlin'.

"He was my first love. I gave him a son, and he *left* me. He got bored. Just like everyone *warned* me he would. We were young, so I figured they didn't know him like I did. Told myself that people change. I told myself he was still figuring out who he was. We were both just teenagers when we got together. I wasn't even seventeen yet when I had Jacoby."

"But he *didn't* change, did he?" I mutter, already knowin' the answer. I've had my fill of trackin' down scorned lovers post-mortem.

She shakes her head. "Nope. Not one bit. My parents tried to warn me. His high school girlfriend tried to warn me. But I didn't listen."

"Look, I get it. He had some sort of *bizarre* charm with women. Sounds like an Ike and Tina Turner song. You were just fools in love. That emotion makes you do some crazy things."

"*I didn't kill him*," she blurts. "I know there were a lot of times I sure as hell *wanted* to. But I loved him *far more* than I hated him."

"I believe you," I mumble genuinely before pointin' at the door Fred blew through a few moments ago. "But Freddy had all hate and no love for the guy, didn't he? Can't be easy watchin' your wife swoon over an old relationship, knowin' you gotta walk a tight wire as long as that man was alive. Word around town is that if you'd have gotten the green light from Carl, you'd have been out that door in a heartbeat."

She doesn't respond. She just pouts and scrubs something on the plank in front of her with the sole of her boot.

"I saw all those messages between you both."

That gets her attention. A look of anger flashes across her puffy face.

"How did you…?"

"Doesn't matter how. But if *I* saw 'em, there's no telling if your hot-tempered hubby'd seen 'em, too. And that's enough motive to commit a heinous crime like this.

Maybe Freddy felt the family he'd built with you was bein' threatened."

"Freddy was *with me* that night. The whole night. Promise. He wouldn't have been able to drive all the way to Killjoy to do something like this without me knowin' about it. We *carpool*, for God's sake."

"Who else might've wanted Carl out of the picture?"

"Just Danielle, his other ex-wife. He said he owed her a ton of money when they split."

"Yeah, I *know*." I can't help but roll my eyes. I feel like a dog chasin' his tail in a big dumb circle.

"She had some insurance policy—"

"Save your breath." I wave a hand and peer down into the gator-infested pit with no railing.

Good Lord, why isn't there railing?!

"I already saw her. She's got an alibi. She *definitely* hated him, but it wasn't her."

"Well, I dunno. Your guess is as good as mine. The only other person I think coulda done it is your daughter. Heard it through the grapevine that Carl had another kid on the way, and I'm not talkin' about the one inside Jolene's belly."

"I know." I feel irritated. I wanted the murderer to be Lisa so bad so I could put an end to this exhaustive search and board my cruise, but that ship has sailed, I guess. I look at my watch. In an hour and forty-five minutes, the Aspire is gonna disembark without me.

"I'm gonna go." I feel defeated.

"Suit yourself." Lisa sniffles.

Thinking about how I might be out of leads to follow up on, I breeze through the preserve, clomping back into the gift shop. I stop cold. Cocodrie is viciously snarling, droolin' like a rabid animal while tryin' to bite a plastic alligator head on a stick, one that clamps its jaws closed with the pull of a trigger. It's a kid's toy. The child holding it is backed into a corner, screamin'. Cocodrie snaps like a shark at the end of his leash, one bein' yanked backward by the lady who sold me my entry ticket.

I approach carefully from behind and take the leash. I pull back, draggin' the Chihuahua's little tan butt backward on the floor toward the door.

"Give me the toy!" I shout. The crying child, a boy about four or five years old, throws the bitin' stick-toy at the floor near my feet. I whirl down and snatch it up just before my mostly blind companion can track it down with his foggy eyes. I look at the lady who works the front desk.

"I told you he don't like kids! Why'd you let one near him?!"

"You're blaming me for that little monster?! Why would you bring that vicious little thing in public at all?! Get out!" She points at the door. "Now!"

I hoist the toy into the air. Cocodrie tugs me around the gift shop in search of it. He's small but powerful. "How much is this?"

"Just go! Take it and get the hell out of here!"

"Fine!" I shout.

"And you had *better* not leave us a one-star review on Yelp for this!" the lady screams, pointin' her finger into the air.

While I want to be offended that I look like the type, let's be real... I had given the idea some consideration. This place hasn't exactly been the epitome of hospitable.

I snap the jaws of the mangled toy in front of Cocodrie's face to taunt my dog and get him to chase it out the front door where there were no children or cranky southern docents furious with me.

I drag the Chihuahua to the back seat of the Buick, open the door, chomp the toy's mouth a few times, and watch the dog hurl himself through the air at it. Despite bein' mostly blind, he still somehow has a weird sixth sense about seekin' out the blood of a perceived enemy.

Once he's in, I toss the toy in and slam the door. He attacks the plastic with a bite force that is *unreal* for such a little dog. I breathe a sigh of relief against the door of the car as it shudders from the scrambling dog's violent attack on the plastic kid's toy inside. Once he feels satisfied that he's destroyed the thing completely, he'll calm down.

Much to my surprise, Freddy is pacing along a fence, cursin' to himself, flailin' his muddy hands wildly. Much like with Cocodrie, I approach with caution. Good Lord, it's not even *noon,* and I've already been around far too many aggressive males today.

"Freddy, you got a second?" I ask, smoothing the sides of my sequined gown down, steppin' around all the rain puddles in the potholes between us.

"What do *you* want? You come over here, poking around, stickin' your nose in where it don't belong, tryin' to play detective."

"I'm jus' tryin' to get some answers, is all."

"Yeah, well, Jacoby said you'd be lurking around here eventually. Said you had Lisa and me on some bulletin board in your room like you work for the FBI or somethin'." He approaches me aggressively. "Lady, I didn't kill Carl Easterly, but I damn sure *wish I had*."

"It's funny, Freddy. I've been hearin' that a lot lately," I say casually, even though he's breathin' in my face. Despite the fact that he's got a good two feet 'a height and at least a hundred pounds of mass more'n me, I'm still not afraid. What's he gon' do, huh? Punch a little old lady?

"If I did know, I'd give the murderer a high-freakin'-five and buy 'em a tank 'a gas as a *thank you* for taking that scumbag out."

"I get it. You have every right to be angry."

He roars out into the humid sky, one full of clouds threatenin' to open up and flood southern Louisiana for the millionth time.

"Lisa was in love with that idiot 'fore I ever even met her. I never stood a chance at dethronin' him as the king of her heart. I wish I could go back and tell twenty-something-year-old Freddy that and shake some sense into my younger self." His arms flap like a bird and slap against his sides. "She'll never love me the same way she loves him. And now the idiot's gone and gotten himself freakin' murdered, which only puts him on this even higher pedestal in her eyes, I'm sure." He flexes his fists, trying to get his anger in check. "...His other ex-wife is gettin' some life insurance payout now. Meanwhile, all Lisa ever got was a broken heart."

"And a *kid*." I cock an eyebrow at him. "Lest we forget about her firstborn."

He rolls his eyes. "I've been paying for that kid ever since he was in diapers, but he always called Carl 'Dad.' The kid wouldn't even go by my last name."

"He made it seem like that was your and Lisa's decision. Not his."

"It sure as hell wasn't *mine*. I *wanted* to claim him! But Lisa... she... wouldn't..." He chews his bottom lip, perplexed as if he's seein' pieces of an invisible puzzle finally fittin' together. "I'll be damned. It was probably her this whole time keepin' Jacoby's last name like that. Like some kind of offering to Carl." His eyes dart up to meet mine. "That's it. I'm gonna leave her. I'm done."

"What?" I panic. The way he looked at me made me feel like I somehow gave him the strength to make the decision, that I somehow just altered their lives forever. "Let's not be *rash*, now."

"No, I'm serious. Holding on to a piece of Carl like that with her son's last name? It makes me sick to think about it. She's been stringin' me around for what... sixteen *years* now? We have our own kids together! And she's in there cryin' over this dead moron, all while namin' the son I raised after that creep. Lord almighty, Carl's *dead,* and he's still ruinin' my life!" His voice shatters the silence of the parking lot, and he hollers loud enough for everyone in the preserve to hear. "The man is worm chow, and she *still* probably loves him more'n me!"

"Calm down." I touch his arm, careful to avoid the smears of caked-on mud. He looks like he's in the middle of a full-body spa treatment. "Relax, Freddy. You're makin' a scene."

"My marriage is over! The man died before he could ever fully break her heart. Don't you get that?"

"I do, but now that he's out of the picture, maybe she'll be more apt to build somethin' with *you.*"

"Aw, horse-crap! Jacoby's about to move out. She's gonna end up turnin' his room into a *Carl Easterly shrine* where she can worship the lowlife for the years to come."

He storms over to a pickup truck with a camper on it and slams down the tailgate. He picks up his utility bag from the ground and angrily slams it inside. It topples, and tools spill out in every direction against the bare metal.

It is at that moment that I see some of them belong to a matching set. The screw-gun was too covered in muck to see it earlier, but they all have perforated yellow grips. On a pair of pliers, I see the same emblem as the one on the hammer at the sheriff's station!

My heart starts to pound.

It's the same strange brand as the murder weapon that killed Carl!

I take a step away from the tailgate, suddenly feeling nervous to be around Freddy. I compose myself. This is exactly the break I needed, after all.

"Nice tools. Been thinking of gettin' me a new set to do all my little projects around the house lately," I lie. "I love the yellow. Say, what brand is that?"

"What?" Freddy looks perturbed to the max.

"You wouldn't know it from the way I'm dressed," I motion down to my black evening gown, "but that shade 'a canary's one of my favorite colors on the planet."

It's another lie. I *hate* yellow. Yellow sucks. Unless it's comin' from a fresh-cut lemon perched on the edge of a cocktail on a cruise ship!

"What's the brand?"

"*Bouchard*. My friend in Lafayette used to make them. Alan Bouchard Tools."

"Where can I get a set?"

He seems extra annoyed at all the questions about his tools. "*Can't*. Bouchard went outta business, like, six years ago."

I reach inside my purse and pull out my wallet. "I'll buy it off ya. What do you want for it?"

"It's not for sale," he growls.

"Everything's for sale, son." I smirk and point back at my car. It is still bobbin' from the canine inside, who is hopefully just still *annihilating* -- and not suddenly making *love* to -- the chompin' gator toy with a force hard enough to bounce the struts. "Don't s'pose you'd wanna trade for a great li'l guard dog, would ya?"

"That thing you came out here with? Pfft. No thanks. I've fed bigger stuff to those reptiles."

I study his loose tools in search of the one that could crack this case wide open. It isn't in or anywhere near the bag.

"Can I see the hammer?" I ask bluntly. "The one that goes with the set? That's the tool I need the most, you know, for hangin' up my karaoke awards and such."

His eyes scan the tools, too. Suddenly, the look on his face changes. His back straightens, and his fists ball up. "Ma'am, who put you up to this?!"

"What? I was just... I just didn't see a hammer. I thought those came pretty standard with a set 'a tools."

"Is Lisa tryin' to pin this on me? Is that what she was tellin' you back there after I left?!"

"No, quite the opposite!"

He grabs his head like his mind's just been blown. "Will she stop at nothing to ruin our marriage?! How could she even think that?!"

"Freddy, I assure you, she didn't!"

But Freddy's mind is miles away. He points to the dirt road, snaking back to the main thoroughfare. "Leave! Leave now, and don't ever let me see your face again, you hear me, you old bat?!"

"Old bat?! I ain't even seventy yet!" I have half a mind to bean this jerk right in his hot head with my purse, but then I remember I got a lot of spare change in here. It'd be like hittin' him with a leather-wrapped brick, and I have no desire to join Carl's killer in the clink.

I stomp over to my Buick and slink inside, feelin' Cocodrie's madness thick in the air. I whip out of my spot (well, more like two spots 'cause I came in hot at a bit of an angle) and drive back to Killjoy, wonderin' if the whole doggone state 'a Louisiana has lost its mind.

21

As expected, the funeral is a classy affair despite the room bein' so small it can only fit thirty people or so. Thankfully, Carl didn't have any real friends, so that thins the attendance down. I suspected, with the exception of Carl's father, Jacoby, Moses Cheramie, my son, Daniel, and my neighbor, Cosmo, the room is otherwise wall-to-wall females, most of 'em past scorned lovers. Still, the decor is beautiful. I expected nothin' less from Cindy after all of the wakes and funerals she's planned in recent years. Still, all of this feels like it's more'n Carl deserves after all the dalliances I've unearthed as of late.

After hearin' several passive-aggressive comments about my sequin gown, I take a seat in the small pew just behind my children.

Daniel has his jaw tensely locked, the edge so sharp you could cut a stick of butter with it. His suit-clad arm is clenched 'round his platinum-blonde wife, Jane. He turns to look at me and forces a weak smile. "Hey, Mama." He reaches back and squeezes my hand. "How you holdin' up?"

My mind flashes to an image of my body curled backward like a rainbow, tryin' not to spill my mojito as I duck under a limbo pole on the Aspire's lido deck. That's what I'd be doin' right now if I weren't stuck here, pretending to pay my respects to a bald cheater who left a trail of angry people wherever he went in life.

"I'm fine, baby." I pat his hand and release it. "Where are the boys?"

Frankly, I am relieved those little hellions aren't here. They'd probably be devisin' a plan to flip the casket and make Carl's heavily made-up face imprint on the carpet. If not that, they'd surely be rigging his arms with fishin' string so they could puppeteer him the second someone came up to pay their respects. *There's something wrong with those kids, I tell ya.*

"Sitter's watching 'em. I didn't need 'em acting a fool on a day like this."

"That's wise." I nod.

"*Mama, you have flour or something all over your dress,*" Daniel whispers. "*Looks like you got in a fight with that woman down at the bakery again.*"

"That was *one time*. She had the nerve to call that monstrous woody log *French bread*. That thing almost chipped my doggone dentures; it was so hard! I was making po boys. French bread's supposed to be light and fluffy. *That thing was solid enough to beat someone to death with!"*

At the last whisper-growled sentence, all my children turn in unison, Jolene flashing me the most disappointing glare of them all. She dabs her eyes with a handkerchief I recognize as her father's. I wave. She glares for a moment and turns back to the casket.

Maggie May strokes Jolene's hair lovingly, and my sister Olivia slides into the pew and shimmies to my right side, her brown eyes fixed straight forward.

"You have *cocaine* on your evening gown, Uma," she growls tensely. "I thought you were off that stuff."

I fight the urge to laugh. "Liv, I gave that up when I found out I was gonna have Daniel. I haven't touched Columbian Marchin' Powder since the *eighties*. And don't say it with so much judgment. Everyone was doin' it back then. Heck, *you* were doing it."

"What is it then? The powder, I mean."

"I had beignets for breakfast."

She nods. "Oh, that makes more sense. Did you get them at Leonard's?"

"No, some li'l place by the hotel. They weren't half bad!"

Olivia scoffs. "Leonard's is the only place I'll eat 'em in Killjoy."

I roll my eyes. "How's Jolene been?"

"She's been goin' through the stages, alright. A bit of rage... a bit of sorrow... all in all, she'll survive. I think findin' out he wasn't Prince Charmin' before they got married will ultimately come out in the wash as a good thing. But you know her. She's as stubborn as a mule. Gets that from you, surely."

I nod, proudly taking credit for that. It's one of my best attributes. "Olivia, I got you a date."

"Oh God." Her posture slumps, and she plops her head in her hands. "I said no more blind dates, Uma."

"He's a decent guy. I've known him forever."

"Lemme guess, you have been tryin' to figure out who killed Carl so's you could go on your stupid cruise. You offered me up like some sacrificial goat for information, didn't you?"

I'm speechless, although I guess I shouldn't be. Olivia's always been astutely observant.

"I'll pay for the date if you just go. Please, Liv," I beg quietly. "I made the man a promise."

"Well, that was stupid, now, wasn't it?" She thinks for a long time. "Fine. But if you're payin', he's gon' take me to that place in the French Quarter I love."

"No. God, Olivia, that's going to be so expensive!"

"Then tell him I'm out."

"I can't! I made the man a promise, Liv. It's one date!"

"Uma, I am not a cheap woman. Maybe that'll teach you to offer me up like livestock next time." She turns to me and speaks quieter. "I want ribeye steak. Raw oyster appetizers. Cocktails. Sauteed mushroom and asparagus up-charges. Desserts. The *whole* nine."

I clench my dentures so hard that the fake teeth might just fall straight out. "Fine! I'm cappin' it at two hundred bucks, though. I'm not goin' into the poorhouse just for tryin' to introduce you to the newest love of your life. He should be buyin' your meal anyway. He's a gentleman."

She scoffs. "It's Wells Anderson, isn't it?"

I don't know how to respond. *Dang, she's good!* I should have just put her on the case of Carl's killer. I'd be halfway to Cozumel by now!

I just sit in silence for a moment.

"In that case, the cap is *three* hundred. And you're givin' me your credit card *before* I go. None of this *reimbursement* crap."

"Fine," I growl.

Olivia smiles smugly and sets her sights on the casket where Carl's pale hands are folded over his large belly. He looks like a wax sculpture of Alfred Hitchcock. "I'm gon' go say a few words so we can get this thing over with. I have bingo at three, and I'll be damned if I'm missin' it over this philanderin' buffoon."

I couldn't agree with my sister more.

Olivia slinks out, and Cosmo slides in by my other side as if they've choreographed this all in some strange dance.

"Well?" he asks expectantly.

"Well, what?" I'm confused. Then, I catch sight of the way his black dress shirt is clingin' to his muscular form, and I lose every thought in my head completely.

"What'd you make of the doorbell footage I sent?"

I snap back to reality. "The file wouldn't play. Bought a new laptop and tried to play it. It kept givin' me and Jacoby a file read error."

"Weird. It should be able to play in most video players."

"Jacoby's been troubleshootin' it. No luck yet."

Cosmo rubs the sexy salt-and-peppered stubble on his jaw and then pulls out his phone. He dials the volume down until it's muted and opens an app. He scrolls down through a library of videos until he finds the one he wants.

"*It hasn't been overwritten yet*," he whispers. "*You can watch it on my phone. It's dark and a bit of a silhouette, but who knows. Maybe it can help you.*"

I watch a video of my house, one in which you get a clear view into my bedroom window as well as my front door and carport. The clip starts with the slow approach of headlights off-screen in front of the Guidry's house. The car's lights click off, and someone gets out and waltzes up the driveway into my carport. The person is tall, stalkin' through the yard with a male's less-than-graceful gait. At the door, the person appears to take somethin' outta his back pocket and look at it for a moment. It's hard to tell from the minuscule size, but I see a flash of yellow, and I imagine it's the hammer.

Though the man's face is too small and shadowed, I picture Fred and the missin' tool at the gator preserve, trying to figure out if the guy in the video could be him.

The person puts the hammer back in a loop of his pants and pulls his shirt down over it. He peers in the window of the carport door. He doesn't knock. Instead, he waves emphatically at someone. A moment later, the door opens wide, and he traipses in. I can see the blur of a person I assume is Carl through the parted sheers in my kitchen and breakfast nook.

Carl appears to offer him breakfast. The person refuses. He's about Carl's height. Similar weight. A moment later, Carl shoves a fishing rod in his hand and points to it. The person appears to examine the rod, eyeing its length, commentin' on the reel.

Finally, the person puts it down, propping it against the wall. Carl takes a seat with what looks like a pile of waffles in the chair I found him dead in. A few moments later, as Carl is seemingly raining syrup down all over his waffles, the person behind him pulls something out from beneath the hem of his shirt.

The hammer.

Oh, Lord.

The second Carl puts the syrup down, the person behind him brings the hammer down.

Once.

Twice.

Carl's head jostles violently with each hit before flopping face-first out of sight. I cover my mouth at the shadowy snuff film I've found myself watchin'.

...At the man's funeral, no less!

The attacker backs up, seemingly shuddering in horror. He covers his mouth and stares at the corpse. Then, the person jostles Carl's body as if he's looking for something.

Suddenly, he hops back in horror, presumably realizin' he's leavin' tracks in Carl's blood. He uses a dish rag to wipe the soles and bolts into the carport. He closes the door carefully and quietly, wipin' his fingerprints from it with the dishrag. Then, the person races off-camera, and the clip ends.

Cosmo takes the phone from my hands and stares up at Olivia as she finishes her vague speech about *what a swell guy* Carl was.

"*Moses has a copy of this?*" I ask Cosmo quietly.

Cosmo nods, never breaking his gaze.

I have so many thoughts all at once. Seein' this could have helped me eliminate Lisa, Melissa, Danielle, and Annie right off the bat, as the perpetrator was definitely male. That tall stature, the wide-set shoulders and hips, the short hair, all unmistakably masculine even through the blur.

In the front row of the funeral, Lisa starts to blubber hard, laying her head on her son's shoulder.

Cosmo leans toward my ear and says, "Who's that? The one cryin' her heart out up front?"

"Carl's first ex-wife."

Jacoby dabs his eyes with a balled-up handkerchief and shudders, wracked with tears himself. Poor kid. Lisa leans up and says something to him that I can't hear and points to his hankie.

"The boy next to her is her son, Jacoby. He's the one who was tryin' to help me get the videos to play."

"Man, that's tough, losin' a loved one so suddenly," Cosmo says. And just like that, my focus turns to how rich Cosmo's voice sounds in my ear. It's like a bold coffee, feels warm and exhilaratin'. "I thought that was her husband this whole time."

I resist the urge to laugh. "No, but I did see *him* this morning. Doubt he'd show his face around here." I lean in closer, close enough to catch a whiff of Cosmo's heavenly aftershave. It makes me forget what I'm about to say for a second.

"Who do you think did it?"

"*I'm almost positive it was that cryin' woman's husband, Frederick Slater.*"

Even though I whispered it, my daughter, Mandy, whips around in her seat and flashes me a warning glare. She whisper-growls back at me. "*Uma, you had better not be trying to play detective again. I know you think you used to help Dad with his cases, but don't you dare go pokin' around with a killer on the loose!*"

Too late.

Mandy faces forward just as Cindy steps in front of the casket and starts readin' some sad poem in Jolene's direction.

"What makes you think it was Fred Slater who did it? I know the guy. He's quick-tempered, sure. But a killer?" Cosmo is whisperin' so close I can smell the mint of the toothpaste he used on that Hollywood smile after eatin' lunch. I'd bet a hundred bucks they're all real, too.

"Well," I lean in, my lips nearly grazing the shell of his ear, "Freddy's got a heck of a lotta motive, watchin' his wife yearn for a man who don't want her all these years. Plus, his alibi ain't exactly water-tight. And he *just so happens* to have a set of tools with the same rare insignia as the murder weapon Cheramie found. It's a company that's no longer around. Can't possibly be a coincidence."

I poke Cosmo's leg, feelin' the firm muscle beneath the fabric. Lord, his body is *hard as a rock*. "He's even got the same build as the guy in your video."

"You gonna go to Cheramie with your theory?"

"Not yet. Not till I'm certain."

"Excuse me," a woman's voice says politely from the back just as Cindy's poem comes to its long-winded conclusion. The woman speaking is peekin' in through two cracked accordion doors, a partition separatin' our tiny parlor from the next one. "Does somebody have a dog outside?"

I perk up. *Crap. What has the little demon done now?*

"A Chihuahua," she says.

I hear the quiet noise of everyone turnin' in their seats to stare at me. I timidly raise my hand. "What's the problem?"

"Well, he gnawed through the leash you had him tied to the water spigot with, and he's runnin' through the cemetery shreddin' flowers now."

"Oh, Lord!" I say as I race out of the room.

***

Half an hour later, I'm covered in sweat and a little blood (my own, I'm fairly certain.) Cocodrie is back in the car, windows cracked, and the guests of the funeral have mostly trickled out to their vehicles. The groundskeeper is currently compiling a lengthy list of headstones whose flowers I am supposed to replace due to Cocodrie's *war on florals*.

Part of me hoped he'd ingested a couple that were toxic so's I could toss the groundskeeper fifty bucks to drop him in the same hole with Carl when they bury him. But knowing my luck, poison would only make the canine stronger and more violent. That dang creature's gonna live well into his twenties just to mess with me. I know it!

Back inside, I sit in silence with Carl's body, the two of us alone for the first time ever. I approach the casket and fight the urge to double over with laughter at the makeup job the mortician did. Carl's cheeks are rosy as a harlot's, and his complexion is far too tan. Inside the casket, there are trinkets. Odds and ends that the living have offered to lay to rest alongside him. There is a monogrammed wedding napkin with today's date. His and Jolene's full names are emblazoned on it in shiny gold foil print. We'd ordered a *boatload* of 'em for the wedding, a wedding that was supposed to be *today*.

"I've been tryin' to find your killer this week, Carl." I snicker. Here I am, talking to a dead man I never really cared for much. "I'll admit, I have been doin' it for my own selfish reasons. You cost me a cruise to the Yucatan. And you cost Jolene a weddin'. You cost all three -- or who knows how many more there might be -- children a chance to grow up with a father they could idolize. You... left all of us one *heck* of a mess."

My eyes graze the trinkets and offerings. There is an old, tattered book of kid's bedtime stories, one that looks like it was popular in the 90s.

I pick it up and flip through it, wondering who it belonged to. Lisa or Jacoby would be my best guess. I riffle through the pages, just wanting to hear the noise of it in my hands. I notice there's a page that wants to separate on its own. I flip to it, realizing that the source of the resistance is a printed four-by-six photograph of a smiling family at Jacoby's high school graduation. He's wearing a black gown and square cap. Lisa is dressed to the nines, a proud mother eager to capture a momentous occasion with a professional photographer against a faux backdrop. Carl is in the picture, too. But he isn't dressed up. He's in a T-shirt that says, 'I don't give a,' and the silhouette of a rodent holding the reigns of a donkey. He looks like he had no idea a photo would be taken. I suspect he was roped into posing for it on the fly. He looks less than enthused, unlike Jacoby and Lisa, who are smilin' so large they almost look like they're under duress.

But as I scan the photo, there's somethin' that catches my eye…

Somethin' that makes my heart *pound*.

Somethin' that blows my investigation into who killed Carl Easterly *wide* open.

I rub my eyes to make sure they aren't deceivin' me, but the picture remains unchanged.

Beneath his long, black robe, Jacoby Easterly is wearin' a pair of black-and-white checkered Vans.

22

I race through the traffic on Airline Highway, doin' a lotta 'Hollywood stops.' Bachman Turner Overdrive is cranked, but I'm the one who is takin' care of business. I fish my phone out of my purse, and Cocodrie growls at me from the passenger seat. I flick the volume knob down, pull up the contact for Moses Cheramie, and press the call button. I swerve, narrowly missin' one of Killjoy's giant potholes.

"Cheramie here. What is it, Uma?"

I always forget that caller ID is a thing, and I stutter over my first few words as I pass someone on the right -- and, by *right,* I mean on the *sidewalk*, but, hey... if there isn't a cop around to see it, is it technically still illegal?

"M-Moses. Did you test the rod for fingerprints?"

"The rod?"

"The fishin' rod. The one propped against the wall behind Carl's body when you processed the scene."

"Look, Uma. I'm assuming this is in reference to Cosmo's doorbell camera footage."

"It is."

"We checked it for prints right away. One set came back to Carl. Another set came back to an unknown. They weren't in the database."

"Could they maybe not have been in the database 'cause they're young and have no priors?"

"Sure… what exactly are you gettin' at?"

I jump a wheel up on a roundabout in the middle of a condominium complex. I'm cuttin' through to take a shortcut to the hotel. "Look, this is going to sound nuts, but… I think our killer might be *Jacoby*."

"Now, why on earth…?"

SCREECH!

I swerve to avoid hittin' a child playin' basketball in a residential driveway. My car whips so hard it nearly goes up on both left wheels. When I look in the rearview, I see I've left a couple nice tire streaks on the asphalt in my wake.

"His stepdad's missin' jus' the hammer from his tool set. I interrogated him about it this morning down at the Gator Preserve in St. Rose."

"Dammit, Uma, I said not to do that!"

I ignore him and keep tellin' him everything I know. "Freddy has the same insignia on all of his tools, but I noticed the hammer was *gone*. Then, at the funeral, there was a book in Carl's coffin, and inside it, there was a picture from Jacoby's graduation. Moses, he was wearin' the checkered Vans! The same ones I saw on Eddie Pickles at the Lagniappe Inn. They were Jacoby's shoes. He must have tried to burn them. It explains why they were found so close to my hotel. That's where he's been stayin' leadin' up to the wedding."

"Why would the boy kill his own father, Uma?" Moses yells, enraged by my digging into the case.

"I dunno, but I'm about to find out! This whole time, I thought he was helpin' me with the investigation to find out who did this to his dad, but now I think he was just doin' it to throw me off with stuff like the *It Was Danielle* letter."

"What letter?"

"After I came to see you at the office, there was a note on my windshield, all ransom-like with the cutout newspaper letters."

"What did it say?"

"Aren't you listenin' to me?! It said *It Was Danielle.* Maybe Jacoby did that to make me spin my wheels a little bit or throw me off the scent after seein' his mama's name on my corkboard."

"Okay. Amos and I'll go talk to him. Bring the ransom letter thing to Clara so we can log it as evidence."

"Come and get it from me at the Lagniappe. I'm headed there to confront the boy right now."

"Don't do that! Uma!"

"Bring backup!" I holler into the phone before ending the call and tossin' it onto the seat by the grumblin' Chihuahua.

"Hang onto your butt, Cocodrie!" I yell as I whip around another corner, goin' just shy 'a double the speed limit.

Cocodrie yips and then hacks up what I can only *hope* is a wad of rose petals onto the floor mat.

23

"Come, Cocodrie!" I stomp my black satin heels on the asphalt of the Lagniappe's parking lot and point to the ground. My heart throbs, poundin' away, makin' me wonder if I could have another stroke over this. The last two were mild. So mild I didn't even know I was havin' one 'til a doctor told me.

Cocodrie sits like an Egyptian sphinx in the seat, paws delicately crossed one over the other, head raised up in a regal pose that says, 'I own this Buick.' A puddle of petal-filled sick sits on the mat below like an offering at the base of a statue. As I lean in to reach for the tattered remnants of his shorn leash, I see blood -- *probably my blood* -- on the snarling gums barely holdin' in his rotting teeth. I snatch up the leash and tie the torn halves together with a box knot (in this moment, I'm grateful that I remember all of the knots Harold so painstakingly taught me durin' our years of outdoor adventures.) I give myself as much distance as possible between the little monster and my flesh, flesh that's already bruisin' from where he bit me at the cemetery.

I give the mended leash a hard tug, and Cocodrie stands at attention, panting his toxic-smellin' breath right in my direction.

"Come on! Yes, I get it. You're the King. I'm your lowly peasant."

That admission seems to satisfy the critter. I don't know if he can understand me or not, but he obliges, hoppin' out of the Buick and craning his wring-able little neck up at the dark, stormy sky.

The wind whips the palm fronds around. Cocodrie and I load into the elevator and ride it up to the third floor. During the short upward trek, he barfs up the head of a Shasta Daisy and then stares forward at the door as if to say, 'Don't look at me. That was already here when I got in.'

We scuttle down the path past my room. I rap frantically on Jacoby's room door. For a moment, I don't hear anything, and I feel a wave of panic rush through me. I start to wonder if he left town to go back to LSU straight from his daddy's funeral.

I knock again. Harder. Louder. *Patience has never been my strong suit.*

"I'm coming! God!" Even though Jacoby's voice sounds angry, I'm relieved I have a chance to confront him now that backup's on the way. The moment I saw the shoes in the photo, I knew in my heart that he killed Carl. All the evidence just makes sense.

The height of the man in Cosmo's doorbell video.

His access to the missin' hammer.

The fact that my door wasn't locked or broken into.

The note on my windshield to throw me off the scent...

But after this week-long quest, I need to know *why*. I've been so focused on evidence and hammers and affairs and camera footage... I never for one second stopped to think that his own son might be the one to take Carl's life.

Jacoby opens the door, and again I get that strange waft of vinegar again. Only this time, it is in addition to...

Cayenne?

I drop Cocodrie's leash and shove my way past Jacoby into his room. I'm a woman on a mission, but I also have to be careful not to show my hand too soon. I might just have to try to be a little crafty if I want a confession.

"Jacoby, I think I figured out who your daddy's killer is."

Jacoby crosses his arms in front of his chest and sniffles. Even though the storm clouds have darkened the sky, his curtains are drawn tight, bringin' a whole new level of dank dreariness to the little box he's called home for a week.

"You did?! Who?"

"I know this is gonna be hard to hear, son. But I'm certain it was your mother, Lisa," I lie. "Now, hear me out..."

I plop onto his bed, quickly takin' note of the mess piled on his floor. Dirty clothes, damp towels, swim trunks, and...

I lift up the towel with the toe of my shoes to see the handkerchief he was wipin' his eyes with at the funeral home slathered with something bright red. At first, I think it might be blood, like from a nosebleed. But then, I realize it's a bit too orange to be dried blood.

So what the heck *is* it, then?

"Your mom claims she loved your dad, right?"

"She *did* love my dad. More'n anything." He says it with defiance, with anger, as if he's correcting somethin' blasphemous.

"She can't be *that* in love with him. She didn't stay single. She married Freddy." Now I'm pokin' the bear intentionally. It's not true, but it might be enough to get a rise out of Jacoby.

"She still loves him. They're going to put him in the ground, and *still,* she's never gonna stop lovin' him. She would *never* kill my father. All she ever wanted was a life with him."

"Right, but..." My eyes dart up to his dresser, where my once-full bottle of Crystal's hot sauce sits nearly empty. It is the same color as the splotches on the handkerchief. I recall the smell of vinegar and cayenne peppers when I came in, and several days ago, too, when he answered the door, eyes red from what I *thought* was from crying. I recall him just hours ago now, dabbing his eyes with a hankie in front of his dad's coffin.

I recall our conversation by the pool a few days back when I insinuated he was takin' his father's death perhaps a little too well.

Did he steal my hot sauce so he could rub it in his eyes and force himself to cry?

"It was Danielle," he finally says, breaking me out of my momentary trance to repeat the words on the ransom-style note verbatim.

Yup, things are startin' to click together more and more.

"Nope, I spoke to Danielle. It wasn't her."

"It was!" he roars, and for the first time, in this young man's presence, I suddenly feel a bit afraid of him. He always seemed like a well-meaning, gentle giant. Now I can see he developed his stepdaddy's temper! "Danielle stood to gain a lot of money if Dad died."

"The policy was only for $125,000, kid. That's really not a life-changin' number these days. It's not like she can retire on that."

"Well, if it wasn't Danielle, it had to be Jolene."

"No," I shake my head and stand, walkin' toward the table in the back of his room. Next to the coffee maker on it, there is strewn trash, a dried-out gluestick, and a folded newspaper with letters ripped out of the headlines. I recognize it. It's the same one his grandparents gave me to pick up Cocodrie's doodie the other morning. He must've snatched it off the top of the trash can!

Clever kid.

I still need to play the part of the clueless idiot, though...

"Here's how I know it's your mom, kid." I pretend to trip on a pair of tennis shoes on my way back to him, splaying dramatically on his bed with a squelched scream.

"Oh God, Gran-Gran! You okay?!"

He rushes to my side to help me up, and I know that even though it would take a monster to kill his own father in cold blood, there is still a nice part of him in there, the part I'd known all week, the part cryin' out for his father's attention as we all sucked down crawfish in my back yard.

"I think... I just tripped on a shoe, is all." I peer at the tag on the tongue of one.

Size 10.

Just like the Vans were.

Its match is sitting next to a pair of the filthiest socks I've ever seen. I picture Jacoby racing through the swampy brush behind the hotel in them as Eddie chased him away from his makeshift bonfire.

Suddenly, a phone rings. But it isn't the hotel phone. It's small and tinny. Jacoby and I both whip our heads to the source of the sound, which seems to be emanatin' from a pile of clothes in the bathroom. Atop the rumpled fabric, I see a cell buzzing around. It has what looks like a Hindu image on it. It's Carl's burner phone, the one for all his affairs!

I look back at Jacoby, and his stance and demeanor change from frightened grandson to obstinate prison guard. His posture says *the jig is up* and that he isn't about to let me leave this hotel room alive.

"He's been more popular than I ever could have imagined this week." Jacoby motions to the buzzing cell phone. "There were so many more women than we even knew about. Women from other states. Women he met online and during vacations. Dating sites galore. Dad was a busy man."

As the phone jingles its final ring, Jacoby turns to the door, nearly tripping on Cocodrie, who is bumbling blindly like a pinball, ricocheting off every low surface in the room. Jacoby pulls the door shut and engages the chain lock on the back of it, sealing us in a cask of darkness. We are dimly illuminated by only a single bedside lamp.

He drags the room's singular chair against the door and sits in it, crossin' his arms and spreadin' his knees in a cocky posture.

"*Jacoby...*"

I don't know what to say. Do I try once more to play dumb, like we both didn't just see a phone Jacoby shouldn't have? Do I try once more to prod with an accusation about his mother? Do I wait for Moses to arrive and just bide my time?

Nah. I'm wayyyyy too nosy for all of that!

I decide on a more direct approach. "You didn't even *try* to get the security footage to play on my laptop, did you?"

He shakes his head unapologetically. "In fact, I scrubbed it from your hard drive after I watched it about a dozen times."

"You wanted to watch yourself murder him again and again? Odd. You never really struck me as the sadistic type."

"I'm not. I watched it to see where I made my mistakes, to see if I could do any more damage control before y'all caught on."

"Makes sense. The weapon could only have been the hammer from Freddy's set, it seems. You had access to that. You had access to anything and everything at Lisa's house." I shrug. "And mine. I always thought it was weird that my door wasn't locked, and yet no one had broken in. But when I finally saw the footage, it made sense that whoever it was was someone Carl let in. What's the deal, Jacoby? You hate catfishin' so bad you'd rather kill your dad than go?"

"Don't be cute. You know it wasn't like that."

"No. I don't. What *was* it like, Jacoby?"

"He didn't even actually want to go with me. I got all the way there at four in the morning, all ready to go fishing with my dad. As soon as I got there, he said something came up and that he had to raincheck me. He showed me his new rod and promised he'd take me soon. But I knew it was a lie. It's always a lie! I suspect he was leaving early that morning to go meet one of his little hussies on the side."

"Sounds on-on brand for Carl." I shrug and then lift up a nearly empty hot sauce bottle. "Nice touch putting this in your hankie and rubbin' it in your eyes to make yourself cry, by the way. That was clever. Although, I'm surprised you didn't blind yourself with as much as you used."

"Well, you said by the pool—"

"Oh, I know. I get it." I point over my shoulder toward the newspaper. "The little ransom note about Danielle was interesting, too. I got a real *thrill* out of seein' that under my wiper. Never pegged you as the arts-and-crafts type."

"I'm full of surprises," he says with malice in his voice.

"Never have truer words been uttered," I say, steerin' clear of Cocodrie as I make my way to Jacoby's bed. Now that we're in dim light, it's like the dog has gained some sort of sixth sense. He's like an angler fish in his element, all fangs and reflective eyes.

"So let me check my work against the teacher's test key, shall we? I wanna see how close I was."

Jacoby shrugs, eyeing me like he's not decided what exactly to do about me yet.

"So… you drive to my house early in the mornin'. Carl lets you in and sits down to eat a plate of waffles, and you club him in the back of the head like some sort of caveman with the claw side of a hammer. Am I right so far?"

"More or less."

"So then, you realize you're trackin' blood. You take off your Vans and even have the foresight to wipe down the doorknob on the way out."

Jacoby looks at the lamp, ashamed.

"Then, you drive back to the Lagniappe and trot off into the swampy little area down 'ere, and you try to burn the evidence. You start yourself a little fire and char that hammer like a hot dog, but you get shooed away, no pun intended, by ol' Eddie Pickles at the front desk, who thinks it's his lucky day, findin' himself a new pair that fits him like Cinderella."

Jacoby's steely eyes return to me.

"The next day, you play dumb. You're there consolin' Jolene and actin' like you wanna help the sheriff in any way possible to find Carl's killer."

He nods. "So far, you're right on the money, Gran-Gran."

God, I hate it when he calls me that.

"You pretended to help me access Cosmo's video file, but instead, you just erased it and said you needed more time. You started stickin' hot sauce in your eyes to fake tears, and you caught a glimpse of my suspect board and panicked. Then, you saw me talking to your real grandparents that next mornin' on the lawn. You knew I was sniffin' around still, so you followed me down to the sheriff's station and stuck that note pointin' the finger at Danielle on my windshield to try to throw me off. Am I still right?"

"Yep. Danielle deserved to be in the hot seat," he says calmly. "Mom was with Dad almost the same amount of years Danielle was. But somehow, the judge gave Danielle some *ridiculous* life insurance policy. What'd my mom ever get, huh?" He rises from his seat, irritated. "All she ever got from that man was heartache!"

"That's all a *lotta* people got from Carl, Jacoby. My daughter included. Seems like the only good thing he ever did was make you and my grandbaby. And, I guess, maybe Melissa's baby, paternity test pendin'…"

"It crushed me, Gran-Gran. It crushed my soul to see how much Mom loved him and how little he ever cared about her. She was just a conquest. She loved him. She would've done *anything* for him, given him the world, gone into more debt, debased herself for his attention…"

"Kudos on using that twenty-dollar word correctly, son, but that still don't give you the right to end a man's life. He was your *father*."

"He was a sperm donor and nothin' more. He never cared about me. When I was a kid and he left, he didn't look back. Not once. He walked out that door like he didn't even have a kid. Never came to school plays. Never helped with a scrap of homework. Never wanted shared custody. Hell, he barely wanted to be at my graduation."

"He didn't look very interested in bein' there in the photo I saw. But still, being a terrible father isn't an excuse for a cold-blooded execution."

"I didn't kill him for being a bad father! This wasn't for me. This was for *Mom*! And *Jolene*! And for all the *other women* he was toyin' with out there."

"I take it you don't regret what you did?"

"Pfft. I regretted it for about ten minutes when I found out he made my birthday the lock code on his real phone. But then, I remembered all the people he's used, and I felt a little justified, frankly."

Cocodrie slams into the nightstand so hard that the lamp wobbles, and I realize his sixth sense was only imagined. I wince at the noise. With a normal dog, I'd rub his noggin, but with Cocodrie, I'd probably draw back a mangled stump if I touched him in this state of confusion.

"Remember a couple months back when I came into town to visit Dad for the engagement party?"

"Vaguely. Kid, that evenin' was a blur. Jolene set up a karaoke machine on the stage and had an open bar. Only thing I remember about that night is about the first three mojitos and a whole lot of me slayin' on stage with the hits of Duran Duran."

"Well, when I visited Mom at the gator preserve, she told me she and Dad were in talks about gettin' back together and that the engagement with Jolene was all a sham."

"It gave you hope that your parents'd get back together, didn't it?"

"Of course it did! All I've ever wanted was to be a family again, for mom to finally be happy and not just wastin' her best years with Freddy."

"Oh, *Jacoby*..."

"That night, I drove to Killjoy, and I followed him all around the engagement party, trying to get *any* time with him that I could. I hadn't seen him in almost a year, and I wanted to talk to him about why he was stringin' Jolene along if he had plans to reconcile with mom... but he acted like he couldn't be bothered. Kept shruggin' me off. Treated me like I was some co-worker of Jolene's that was just there for the free shrimp bar."

"Oh," I rub my stomach, forgetting for a moment that I'm in the presence of a cold-blooded murderer, "I *do* remember that. That poor caterer fella couldn't de-vein those gulf shrimp to save his life."

"Dad went outside for a bit. I followed him, hopin' that if I got him alone, we could talk. I cornered him out there by the bushes and started firin' off questions. I didn't know how long I could keep his attention."

Jacoby looks like he is about to cry actual tears now, ones not caused by rubbing cayenne peppers into his eyeballs.

"He called Mom *delusional*. Said he had no plans of ever gettin' back with her. He said he loved Jolene and that she was the only woman for him. Then, his cell phone rang."

He points to the phone in the hotel room with the Hindu God, Shiva, emblazoned on it.

"Not his regular phone, but *that* thing. He cut me off to take the call, and he started flirtin' with some other girl right there in front of me! Right at his and Jolene's engagement party! Right after my mom said he wanted to get back together with her! I couldn't believe it. He tried to play it off like it was a work phone at first, and then when I told him I wasn't stupid and that I knew it wasn't a work call, he jokingly confessed that *what a woman doesn't know won't hurt her*."

In a violent burst of energy, Jacoby smashes a standing lamp against the wall, shattering the bell on top into frosted shards that patter onto the dingy carpet. Cocodrie looks in the wrong direction to see if he can assess the source of the noise.

"But that's all these secrets ever do! They hurt them!" Jacoby weeps freely. "If he didn't want to get back with my mom, that's fine. But *Jolene* was nothin' but nice to him. She didn't deserve that. She always paid me far more attention than he *ever* did. She was ready to take me on as a step-mom even though she's just a few years older'n I am!"

"Jolene's a good person. Her compass is a little off-north sometimes, but ultimately, she wants the best for people. I think she really loved your Dad. Hell, she was still at his funeral today even though she'd found all kinda love letters he'd been writin' to other women."

"Yeah," Jacoby ruffles his dark hair, the sole thing that sets him visually apart from being a younger carbon copy of his dad. "At the party, I saw how he was actin' with Melissa. Then, I saw her new infant, one that looked eerily similar to my *own* baby pictures. I didn't know how far his cheating went, but I knew that Dad was a *menace.* I couldn't stand around and let Jolene end up just like my mom. Someone had to stop the cycle. My mother is stuck in limbo. Has been for decades. And she probably *will be* forever now. She's stunted. She compares everything to the way *Dad* used to do it. I thought about the baby in Jolene's belly growin' up with the same exact Dad I had, one who wouldn't give it the time of day, one he'd surely just walk out on in a few years. I had to do somethin'. He wasn't gonna stop."

"You're right about that," I say.

Jacoby starts to pace erratically. "The other night when I got into town, Dad said he wanted to go see a movie with me. I got to the theater and he never showed, Uma."

I shake my head. "Shameful."

"So I went to visit Mom and Freddy that night, I was revved up. I saw Freddy's tools there and I just…"

Jacoby doesn't finish his sentence. He just paces some more, remindin' me of a ticked off zoo animal wantin' out of its cage.

"Carl was a terrible person, Jacoby. I can't argue that. There were way too many people payin' him undeserved respect at that funeral today, in my opinion. But you got your whole *life* ahead 'a you, kid. He sure as heck wasn't worth jeopardizin' all that."

Jacoby roars and then folds over into a sob.

Just then, Carl's second phone rings again. Flustered, the tall nineteen-year-old races into the bathroom to pick it up. "This thing's been goin' off nonstop all week! How many half-brothers am I gonna end up findin' out about when all is said and done?!" Jacoby hurls the burner phone at the wall.

As it explodes, shatterin' into pieces, I leap off the bed, climb atop his chair, and unlatch the door. Just as I'm gettin' down, Jacoby returns, spannin' the distance between us in two huge strides. He hooks an arm around my waist and hoists me into the air like I'm a pillow.

Cocodrie barks at the commotion, seething with anger. *For whom, he isn't sure.* But the fury is there, brewin' in him as he waddles out and stands behind Jacoby.

While I'm hoisted in the air, I slam my feet against the door near the peephole, launchin' Jacoby and I back through the room. Cocodrie yips as Jacoby trips over him, and we slam to the ground. Fortunately, the boy catches my fall. Otherwise, I'd have probably snapped a doggone hip!

I try to wrench myself from Jacoby's grasp, but it's too tight. That is, 'til he clocks Cocodrie in the face with a flailin' socked foot, and the dog attacks with all his might, tearing at his toes through his filthy socks with fervor. The attack gives me just enough time to climb to my feet with a strained grunt. I hobble to the door, topple the chair over, and scramble out onto the third-floor balcony.

The rain is comin' down again in sheets as another tropical storm band bears down on Killjoy. My screams for help are carried away on the wind whippin' through the complex. In the distance, through gray precipitation pourin' down like God left a faucet wide open, I see the flash of red-and-blue lights atop one of the Killjoy sheriff's vehicles.

I hear Jacoby scream and kick the dog. That only seems to enrage the ancient Chihuahua more. Jacoby scrambles toward the balcony, hot on my trail. I wave to Deputy Amos Landry on the ground level as he makes his way through the pool area, but I feel Jacoby's hands clasp around my throat before I can squeeze out any sort of cry to accompany it. The fingers tighten down, and I feel the edges of my vision blur, vignetting into darkness. My pulse throbs in my skull. I feel the panic of impendin' death rush through me, the kind that, if I were an animal, it'd taint my meat and make me dang-near inedible.

I hear a familiar voice beside me. "Hey! Get your hands off of her!"

As my face fills with blood and my fingers claw at Jacoby's, I feel him jerk me to the side and roar out in pain. His grip loosens around my neck, and suddenly I suck in a humid gasp of air, clutchin' my chest as it fills with sweet oxygen. As I back away toward the dead end of the third floor's path, I turn to see Eddie Pickles with Jacoby in a chokehold.

Jacoby has to have dang-near a hundred pounds on the scrawny hotel manager, but what Eddie lacks in size, he seems to make up for in scrappiness, thank God!

Cocodrie is still latched onto Jacoby's ankle, flying around with every kick. Bloody footprints are bein' stamped through the rain all over the concrete outside Jacoby's hotel room.

Eddie has latched on tight, tryin' to get Jacoby to pass out. Amos is booking it up the three flights of stairs, and Moses is yelling from the pool deck. I can't tell what he's sayin' through the downpour.

Cocodrie shreds more of Jacoby's skin with the most violent noise I've ever heard him make. Jacoby screams and then lands a punch in Eddie's belly, one accompanied by the crunch of ribs. Eddie growls in pain and whips Jacoby's awkwardly tall frame over the railing.

I scream as Jacoby topples over the side, a perilous thirty-foot drop.

Cocodrie never lets go, sailing through the air with the boy into the rainy abyss for what is certain to end in either instant death or paralysis.

Eddie's and my screams are cut short by the *slam* of a body onto a plastic lounge chair by the edge of the pool. It collapses upon impact and is followed by a massive *splash* as Jacoby and Cocodrie plunge into the water.

Still gasping for air, I study the look of horror on Eddie's face, mouth agape in pure shock that he might have just killed someone in an attempt to save us both. But seconds later, I hear Jacoby roar in pain.

"Jacoby Easterly, you're under arrest! Get out of the pool!" Moses screams, department-issued pistol aimed at Jacoby's chest as he flails clumsily toward the shallow end.

Miraculously, Cocodrie paddles, his little fawn-colored feet kicking like he's in some kind of girly slap fight. Tendrils of red trail behind his mouth like he's spittin' up pomegranate juice in the chlorinated water.

Rain batters us all, and I slump to the concrete, tenderly cupping my bruised neck and staring up at Eddie with gratitude.

"I owe you big time, Pickles," I say through a scratchy throat, unable to hide my smile.

"He missed checkout earlier and wouldn't let the maid in. I was coming to evict him."

"Remind me not to ever ask *you* for an extension." I laugh.

Eddie helps me up and steadies me as we make our way down the flights of stairs. Amos shoves Jacoby through the wall of water that's gushin' off the rooftop. He presses the boy into his squad car, making sure Jacoby doesn't slam his head as he slips inside, all soakin' wet and handcuffed.

Moses frowns at me. "Uma Mae Blanchard, I *told* you to wait!"

"I'll keep 'at in mind next time I confront someone 'bout bein' guilty of patricide."

Moses tucks beneath the overhang to avoid the gutter splash. "Eddie, grab us a few pool towels, would ya?"

"Sure," Eddie says before boltin' obediently through the rain toward the office.

Once we are alone, Moses looks at me with compassion. "You alright, Uma?"

I nod. "I got a *lot* to tell you, and I'm starvin'. Can we do all the paperwork and stuff down at the station?"

"Of course. I'll have Clara order up some dinner."

Just then, the soft *plunk* of little feet in the shallow end of the pool grabs my attention. Cocodrie shakes the water off and trembles, a look of hatred filling his foggy eyes.

"Whoops. Best not forget the dog," Moses mutters, jogging out toward the canine. He reaches in to grab the dog.

"Careful!" I shout. Just as I do, Cocodrie snaps at him with a demonic gurgle. Moses nearly slips and falls backward, catchin' himself on a bent knee just in time.

"Only grab him by the leash. That mouth-end is deadly."

Moses looks back over his shoulder at me. "You really should think about puttin' a muzzle on this thing."

"He and Pickles just saved my life. This is how you talk to a hero?"

I fight the urge to laugh as I watch a beefy Sheriff in his forties timidly retrieving a wet dog the size of a football from the water. The thought of a muzzle on that dog makes me wanna laugh aloud. He'd look just like a tiny Hannibal Lecter in it.

Then again, I guess *that'd* be kinda fitting.

24

A few months came and went. Word on the street is that Jacoby's all set to take some kind of plea deal for the murder of Carl. I've visited him a few times there at the jail. While it wasn't nice of him to try to kill me, I still felt a little sorry for the kid. All he ever really wanted was a little attention from his parents. Now, neither will talk to him. One's dead, the other's angry that he killed the love of her life.

The poor boy just couldn't catch a break even though, in my eyes, he also sorta did the world a *little* bit of a favor.

Was it too extreme? *Absolutely.*

Did his ol' man have it comin'? Well, let's just say, if Jacoby hadn't done it, Carl was on a path to end up in the same place at the hands of someone else, whether it be over jealousy, too many donuts, or impregnatin' the wrong man's wife.

Danielle paid off her house with the insurance money. Clara said her girlfriend's already shackin' up with her. Good for Danielle.

Eddie Pickles was recognized in the paper for his heroic feat. About a month ago, I started invitin' him out to karaoke with my sisters and me. Finally, I have someone to do the duets with now. Eddie does a mean Meatloaf impression in *Paradise By the Dashboard Lights*.

Cindy still talks about the funeral like it was a wedding. She's even been tryin' to get a part-time job at the funeral parlor plannin' 'em. I'm curious to see how that's gonna pan out.

Olivia finally went out with Wells. The dinner cost me $327 dollars. She claims she wants no part of datin' him, but I saw him riding his Harley down Airline the other day with a woman on the back. Even though the helmet was obscurin' her face, I can recognize my older sister from a mile away. It was *definitely* her.

Cocodrie survived the fall, unfortunately. The little vampire turns sixteen in two months. He's still got an affinity for the taste of blood.

Things with Jolene haven't quite been the same since Carl died. She's been cold and aloof. Barely wants to talk to me, as if I somehow took part in the man's murder. I guess she's still upset that I was a little more focused on the cruise than helping her plan a funeral.

Speakin' of the cruise…

I look at the digital ticket's QR code on my phone. I board a massive vessel for a five-day, four-night trip to the Yucatan next week!

Finally, I'll be able to relax with a mojito in one hand and a microphone in the other. And due to the delay, my son's whole family and Cosmo are gonna join me so's we can celebrate my sixty-ninth birthday aboard the Oshannic Aspire. It is gonna be glorious after all this wait. Plus, you know, on vacation, nothin' can go wrong.

ABOUT THE AUTHOR

Trixie is an award-winning author and filmmaker, an artist, a film industry grip, and a cancer survivor. Born in Wyoming, she spent most of her adult life in central Florida and southern Louisiana. She now lives on the beach in Connecticut. When she isn't writing or reading, she is tending her massive vegetable garden, solving cold case files with her younger sister, singing her heart out at karaoke, or kayak fishing.

Trixie Fairdale is a cozy mystery pen name (an easy way to keep her various genre fiction separate for readers.) She has also published award-winning horror and fantasy under her real name, Erica Summers. She also writes contemporary romance under the pen name Odessa Alba.

ACKNOWLEDGMENTS

First and foremost, I would like to thank my sister and business partner, **Heather Wohl**. You are so strong and beautiful. Without your encouragement, I would not be a fraction of what I am. I love you.

Dave Sikora, you are the love of my life. Thank you for always rooting for me and supporting every hair-brained shenanigan I come up with. You are always in my corner and always there with a "you *GOT* this" whenever I need it. I love you so much.

Chisto Healy, you are an amazing author and friend. Thank you for your continued support.

To **Wells Smith**, you are truly such a character. I miss my days of being on movie and television sets with you. I just had to make other people love you, too.

To **Ryan Watson** for all the crawfish boils and great convo over cold Coors.

To **Eddie Sampson**, may you rest in peace. I will never forget about you, and I hope wherever you are, you enjoy being part of my wild, fictional adventures still.

To **Jana DeLeon** and **Toby Neal**, your cozy mysteries are an inspiration to me. I love your style.

And **Lindsey Holt**, you are the most voracious champion of my books under every pen name, an adoring fan, and a wonderful person. You are living proof that not all heroes wear capes. You will never know how much your support has meant to me. Thank you for all that you do to unite our books with readers everywhere.

A Note From The Ogres

Even though this book was proofread thoroughly by professionals, beta readers, and ARC readers… mistakes happen. We want our readers to have the best experience possible. If you spot any spelling, grammatical, or formatting errors, please feel free to reach out to us at:

Rustyogrepublishing@gmail.com

Reviews

If you could take the time to leave an honest review after you've read this book, we would greatly appreciate it. We respect your time and promise it doesn't have to be long and eloquent. Even a few words will do!

As a small publishing house, every review helps others determine if this book is right for them and greatly increases our chances of being discovered by someone else who might enjoy it.

COMING SOON:

MORE RUSTY OGRE MYSTERY:

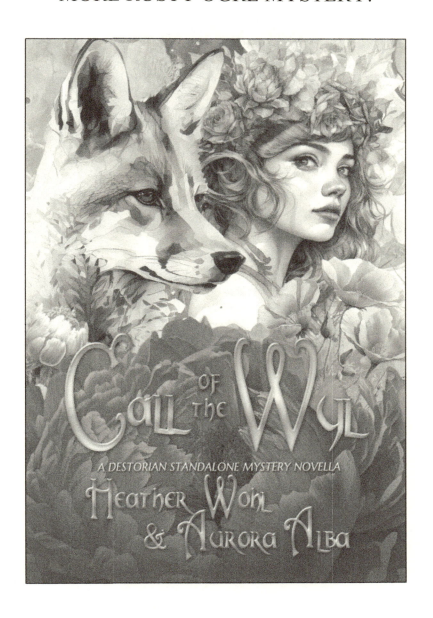

Made in the USA
Las Vegas, NV
01 August 2025